There is a song with the lyrics 'words come easy'. Words did not come easy to Ken Wise until rather late in his life – in retirement to be precise. Despite that, Ken felt inspired by the adventures he'd had spending the early part of his life in the United States Air Force. Circumstances then led Ken to move to Spain where he decided to write first novel, *A Limey in the Court of Uncle Sam*.

Ken consequently became hooked on the written word. He has since written two novels, one being *Estate Agents Beware*, a refreshing contrast to his first book.

KEN WISE
ESTATE AGENTS BEWARE

SilverWood

TORFAEN COUNTY BOROUGH		
BWRDEISTREF SIROL TORFAEN		
01626602		
ASKEWS & HOLT	04-Sep-2012	
AF	£8.99	

Published in paperback 2012 by SilverWood Books, Bristol, BS1 4HJ
www.silverwoodbooks.co.uk

Copyright © Ken Wise 2012

The right of Ken Wise to be identified as the author of this work
has been asserted by him in accordance with the Copyright,
Designs and Patents Act 1988.

All rights reserved. No part of this publication may be reproduced,
stored in a retrieval system, or transmitted in any form or by any means,
electronic, mechanical, photocopying, recording or otherwise,
without prior permission of the copyright holder.

This is a work of fiction. Names, characters, places and incidents either
are products of the author's imagination or are used fictitiously. Any
resemblance to actual events or locales or persons, living or dead, is
entirely coincidental.

ISBN 978-1-78132-004-4

British Library Cataloguing in Publication Data
A CIP catalogue record for this book is available from the British Library

Set in Sabon by SilverWood Books
Printed on paper sourced responsibly

*To Christine, my wife,
who has been subjected to countless proof reading sessions
also with thanks to my editor, Carol Cole*

Chapter One

Tom Rendell turned into the autoroute service area just outside Paris, stopped and peered intently at his road atlas. He had been driving around for hours and already it was beginning to get dark. He switched on his interior map light and looked again at the directions given to him by Trisha, his slender, red-haired secretary, who had answered the telephone call from France. As usual, she had given him only the most basic information. His handsome face creasing in a puzzled frown, Tom ran his fingers through his curly dark hair and heaved a sigh of frustration. This could not be correct: the road he had conscientiously followed had led to nowhere. If only he had used the Merc instead of the BMW; at least he would have had the sat nav to make his task a little easier.

He parked up, eased himself out of the car and stood for a moment, shivering. The keen March wind had seemingly followed him across on the overnight ferry from Dover. Glancing up at the restaurant area, Tom hesitated. Trisha would be waiting for his call, but he fancied something hot to eat. Locking the car, he set off briskly towards the beckoning lights and positioned himself at the end of the line that would lead him to the cooked meal section. He would have to find a cheap B&B for tonight; then he would contact Trisha and get her to call Madame Connie Pasteur who had telephoned his office yesterday. Evidently the Frenchwoman wanted to discuss with him the disposal of her property; hence this unscheduled trip to France.

Waiting in the queue, Tom's thoughts turned to work. Over the years his estate agency had prospered and, having now reached the age of forty-one, he had branches in London, Paris and Rome, admittedly keeping only a small staff in each one: an assistant to manage the office, answer the phone queries and deal with the mail. He spent most of his time at his Windsor office. He had moved out of the City some time ago, relocating his base to premises near the castle and living in a village close by. He had been lucky in his staff: Jessica in Paris and Cassie in Rome. Both women had worked for him a long time and were the sole survivors of the heyday when the property market had boomed. It was different now; estate agents had to have some money behind them to survive. Most were still reeling from last year's recession and trying desperately to recover. Tom himself had been forced to consider closing the Paris and Rome offices but, having a soft spot for both girls, he had dismissed the idea – he was not that desperate yet.

As he waited in the busy line, an image of Jessica popped vividly into his mind. Some years ago he'd had something of a serious fling with the dark-haired beauty whose voluptuous figure had always drawn admiring looks when she had accompanied him on their customary evenings out in Paris after work – evenings that inevitably ended in his hotel bed that he should be so lucky!

And then there was Cassie. Fair-haired, petite and extremely pretty, she had recently divorced her Italian husband whom she had married shortly after leaving college. The divorce had surprised Tom – they had seemed such a well-suited couple – but this had never stopped him from dropping hints that he was always willing to mix business with a little pleasure should this appeal to her. Much to his disappointment, her usual response had been one of cynical amusement which had left him wishing he had not made his play. It was some time now since he had bothered to try but one of Tom's favourite sayings was that 'nothing stays the same'. He also knew that the staff kept in close touch with each other by phone and doubtless his love trysts had been relayed many times in their weekly calls. He chuckled ruefully; it seemed the fairer sex were not much better than men when it came to brightening their days with bits of salacious gossip.

'And for you, Monsieur?'

Tom was brought up short. He had reached the end of the queue and the rather pretty girl behind the counter was waving a serving spoon and looking him up and down with an inquisitive expression.

'Sorry, I was miles away.' Treating her to a beaming smile, he selected a dish of French sausage and fries with an ample amount of bread. He collected a bottle of beer from the cool rack at the end of the counter and moved on to the cash desk. No matter which country you were in, motorway services always seemed the same: some more rough and ready than others, but nevertheless essential to the hungry traveller.

As he ate his meal, Tom looked out idly at the darkening skyline, and spotted the illuminated sign of a hotel chain he knew. Good – he would not have to travel far for his overnight stay; well, at least he hoped not.

Trisha Andrews kicked off her shoes and went to the fridge, took out a couple of eggs and some tomatoes to make a quick omelette. She had waited at work for the inevitable call for help from her boss, knowing only too well that Tom would be likely to do two things. Firstly, he would miss the sign that would take him to his intended destination and secondly, he would misread just about everything else. She had given him the usual strict instructions to telephone her on his arrival so she could fill in the gaps before he went to the property to meet the client. She might as well not have bothered. Trish often wondered how Tom Rendell had done so well over the years; he was always so forgetful about names and addresses.

She had waited in vain; time passed and there had been no phone call. Giving up, she travelled home in order to feed Sandy, her Persian cat, have something to eat, and put her feet up.

Tom's timing was, as usual, way out; the call came just as she was about to take her second mouthful of the delicious omelette.

'Hullo, Trish.' He sounded cheerful enough.

Trish grimaced; the late call could mean only one thing: predictably, her boss had got himself lost. The man was hopeless! 'Hullo, Tom,' she echoed.

'Where are you now?'

'At home. More to the point, where are you?' Trish tried and failed to keep the irritation out of her voice.

'Um, I got a bit lost,' Tom offered in a placatory tone. 'Can you contact Madame Pasteur and explain that I have been unavoidably delayed and will see her first thing in the morning?'

'OK,' Trish agreed. 'I'll call you back.' Taking down Tom's exact location she ended the call, threw her now rubbery omelette in the bin and dialled the Frenchwoman's number.

Tom had just booked into his room at the Champion Hotel and poured himself a drink from the mini-bar when his mobile rang and Trisha's customarily pained tones sounded in his ear. 'I've spoken to Madam Pasteur and she said you are only minutes away from her. She's made special arrangements for the meeting and asks that you make the effort to get to the house tonight.'

'Oh Lord,' Tom groaned, eyeing up the comfortable bed, 'must I?' He had been looking forward to a shower and an early night but, from what little information he had gleaned from Trisha, he knew this could be a good instruction to get. 'OK,' he sighed, 'tell her I'll be there shortly. Can you give me the exact directions again?'

Exactly fifteen minutes later, Tom arrived at his destination. It was certainly close; in fact he must have driven straight past the entrance earlier. His eyes lit up: the property was huge; a *grand château* – almost as large as Windsor Castle. Well, perhaps not quite that grand!

The two big ornamental gates opened invitingly without him having to get out of his car. Tom drove up the wide drive and parked in one of the many parking spaces illuminated by security lights in front of the château. Straightening his tie and smoothing down his hair, he walked up to the main entrance and pulled on the hanging bell rope. At first he heard nothing beyond a distant jangling, but suddenly one of the great doors swung open and a woman's voice invited him to step inside. She had spoken in perfect English which came as a pleasant surprise.

'Madame Pasteur?' Tom queried, peering at her intently and extending his hand. 'Tom Rendell... you should have received a call from my secretary? Please accept my apologies; I was unavoidably delayed.'

In the dark interior a number of candles burned brightly, but their overall effect seemed rather lost in such a large area. Tom could just about make out an impressive staircase rising from the hallway and concluded it must lead to bedrooms on the next floor, though how many he could not hazard a guess such was the immense size of the property. As his eyes grew accustomed to the gloom, he turned his attention to his hostess and was gratified by what he saw. French women certainly knew how to present themselves in a most seductive way. He quickly put aside any thought that this was for his benefit. He knew from experience that Continental women – perhaps even more than British women – dressed well as much for their own pleasure as to attract members of the opposite sex. Either way, Tom could not help but show his appreciation. Connie Pasteur fitted his image of a sophisticated Frenchwoman to a tee, right down to the delightful swell of the ample bosoms revealed by her low-cut, well-fitted dress. Her hair glinted in the candlelight and, although worn short, seemed to fit nicely with his initial impression that this was indeed a lady of class.

'Ah yes,' she said softly, her hand lingering in his, 'there is no need to apologise. Your secretary has only just called.'

Tom noted that this glorious creature had incredibly green eyes and that she was allowing her gaze to drift over him, her gorgeous lips lifting in a slight smile of invitation – but surely he must be imagining her look of satisfaction?. He stared at her curvaceous form, becoming aware that she seemed happy to let him have his fill. 'Please come through,' she murmured, bringing the mutual appraisal to an end and sweeping past him, intoxicating him still further with the fragrance of her perfume. He had no idea what it was but, as she led him across the hallway and into a spacious lounge, he visualised it being sprayed completely and sensuously over her body.

The log fire burning in the enormous grate was impressive. Numerous sets of candles located on the walls of the grand lounge flickered invitingly, adding to the amazing overall effect of a film set for a costume drama. Tom wondered briefly if there had been a power cut, until he remembered the security lights.

Motioning him to come closer, Connie bent over a low satinwood table to pour him a drink from the crystal decanter resting there. The backdrop of the fire and softness of the lighting seemed only to increase the woman's voluptuous magnificence. Tom gulped. Surely this vision before him could not possibly be wearing anything beneath her incredibly tight-fitting dress?

Tom sipped the large glass of neat Scotch she handed him, gasping as it hit the back of his throat. Any thought of having an early night at his meagre hotel was consigned immediately to the waste bin. Determined to enjoy what fate had thrown him, he became aware that his hostess was speaking and, reluctantly dragging his gaze from her cleavage, he forced himself to focus on the purpose of this meeting.

'I have to apologise, Tom... oh, do you mind if I call you Tom?'

Speechless, Tom shook his head. He knew full well that if she had called him Fido he would have responded.

Connie smiled. 'When I asked you to come over tonight, I was quite unaware of how late it had got. I hope you will forgive me.'

Tom swallowed. Good grief! All this was beyond his wildest dreams and the woman was apologising?

'I don't feel like talking business tonight,' Connie was saying, 'and I'm sure you must be tired. If it is alright with you, we can continue in the morning after breakfast. You must of course stay the night. I would not dream of letting you drive back to the hotel having dragged you here on a fool's errand.'

Still speechless, Tom nodded enthusiastically to indicate that he would welcome anything she proposed. Anything!

'Please, do sit down,' Connie beckoned, sinking into a large white armchair and gesturing to a similar one that faced her on the opposite side of the fire.

'Thank you,' he managed. Attempting not to notice the

glimpse of slender leg peeping out through the slit in Connie's dress – a slit which he could have sworn had not been there before – Tom did as he was told and tried to pull himself together. Enfolded in the soft comfort of the armchair, he began to relax. Madame Pasteur had suggested nothing improper and it made sense for him to stay over if that was what she wanted – wasn't that so? It occurred to him, as he sipped his whisky, that the dream might be shattered at any moment by the sudden appearance of the man of the house. There must surely be one. A woman like this could not possibly live alone – could she?

As if she had read his mind, Connie started to relate her circumstances. In fact she was a widow. She had married at an early age and had lost her husband to a heart attack five years ago. Murmuring the customary sympathetic phrases, Tom assumed Monsieur Pasteur had been an older man and could well imagine this woman causing a fatal response in a man past his prime. 'Get a grip, Tom,' he told himself.

Grace personified, Connie rose from her chair, picked up the whisky decanter and refilled his glass, her eyes maintaining contact with his as she filled it to the brim without spilling a drop. This lady had perfect balance; that was for sure. Tom's gaze drifted to her breasts, which seemed to swell even further as if in an attempt to burst forth.

Tom shook his head furiously and Connie laughed. 'Oh, I am sorry, Tom, is it too hot in here? Please, take off your jacket.' She stepped back to allow him to remove his jacket. That was certainly better; he felt the warm glow of the fire take over his right side and he loosened his tie a little.

Connie stepped forward. 'Tom, you are still too hot and I am forgetting my manners, please let me help you.' With that, she expertly pulled Tom's tie apart and let it drop to the floor.

What happened next felt like it was happening in slow motion; he found his shirt being unbuttoned, leaving his chest exposed to the warm glow of the fire. He instinctively put his hands out, as if to... he didn't know what, but suddenly he found that his hands were touching soft flesh! Connie Pasteur had disrobed in what could only be described as the quickest dress change he had ever witnessed – the only difference being that she was not putting on anything else to replace it.

Tom could not believe what was happening as he felt himself being pulled forward. He dropped to his knees onto the soft white rug which ran the length of the fireplace and he found to his delight that his initial impression of the lady having nothing on under her dress was correct in every way...

Trish put her phone down and cursed silently; no answer, again. She could only hope that her boss had managed to negotiate the simple task she had set him. She knew that the deal could possibly be a good one and she hoped that Tom, her boss of ten years, would not mess it up by not turning up. He had the experience to give a client what they wanted and the company always needed to keep ahead in these difficult economic times.

She went upstairs and stepped into the shower, letting the warm water gently cascade over her ample breasts which, along with her exquisite figure, were perfectly formed. Trish always kept herself in the best of fitness; swimming daily and going to keep fit four times a week. Trish prided herself that, by keeping herself in top form, her lover would not have the need to wander from the family home. It had taken many of her feminine ways to get her boss to commit to moving in with her five years ago, but it had been worth all the effort.

Finishing her shower she put on her slinkiest nightdress.

She would miss her boss that night but it was a small price to pay if the company could obtain the order. As she lay in bed missing Tom, she had no idea that, miles away, in an equally large bed, her lover and boss was giving it his all.

Chapter Two

Just outside Windsor, Trevor Miles was pulling into the long driveway of his large detached property. He had left the office early that afternoon so he could get back at a reasonable hour to spend some time with his children. After four days away in London, he was ready for some home comforts. An unassuming man in his mid-forties, his hair already thinning on top, Trevor gave everyone the impression of being your everyday accountant: a man to be trusted with your money and the last person you would take to be the high-flying, successful stockbroker that he was.

With a crunch of gravel, he swung the Daimler in front of the house and applied the handbrake. He could not be bothered to put the car away tonight and, anyway, it was perfectly secure; the gates were always locked by the groundsman before he retired to the lodge at the entrance to the impressive grounds. Trevor had purchased the property from an impoverished aristocrat who had long given up trying to keep the spacious house and grounds in the manner which it richly deserved.

Allison, Trevor's pretty fair-haired wife of ten years, met him at the door and gave him a welcome home kiss. She missed him when he was away but he was rarely gone for more than four days at a time and she enjoyed the fruits of his labours, which was some compensation, he supposed. Returning her kiss, he noted with some satisfaction that she had kept all the attributes that had attracted him to her all those years ago, when he first met her at a mutual friend's birthday party. Despite presenting him with three children, her figure was as trim, her complexion as flawless, and her blue eyes still held that glint which had made him putty in her hands.

Moments later, Trevor was being mobbed by their offspring. He had promised that this weekend they would all go to the seaside, and their excitement was building to fever pitch. After sitting down to a light meal, he quietened his clamouring kids with the obligatory bedtime stories then settled down with his wife in front of the television. Allison had learnt never to ask him how his week had gone, probably because he had always brushed aside any questions about his work. As she had once said, 'Evidently nothing really exciting happens in a stockbroker's world of commerce, darling!' Laughing, he had not troubled to disillusion her.

With Allison snuggled contentedly beside him relating all that had taken place during his absence, Trevor began to doze. Watching television always had that effect on him.

Cassie Carlota arrived at her office just as the rain stopped. She shook her shoulder-length fair hair and entered the small office, stopping briefly to check that the make-up she had applied earlier was still in place. She applied the scantiest of lip gloss just to ensure she would be at her best in case any potential clients chose to wander in from the street. Cassie Carlota always liked to be at her best whatever the time of day or night.

She had travelled the short distance from her home, stopping only at the local bakery to buy her usual takeaway breakfast of coffee and croissant. Now she eyed the unopened post and decided it could wait until she had finished her meal. Cassie had been working many years for the handsome English boss who came to visit her approximately once a month. However, she was not a person to dwell on the past and she now looked forward to new relationships and eventually, perhaps, finding someone to share her life with. One thing was for sure: she knew she would not be accepting any of Tom's numerous invitations to wine and dine each time he visited her. She had no problem with lunchtime meetings but normally, after a long business session chasing up the leads she had acquired the previous month, the only time she had left for socialising was late in the evening. Cassie had always relied on being married to excuse herself from accepting her handsome boss's dinner invitations. It had enabled her to ward off his advances – for advances they were, stopping just short of an actual invitation to take their business relationship further. She had enough experience to know when a man was coming on to her and had always made it plain to Tom that she knew of his dalliance with Jessica in Paris. However, she often wondered just how long her resistance could last. After all, she was now single in every sense and he, well he did have that certain *je ne sais quoi*. Either way, it would be two more weeks before she had to face him. She turned her attention to the post and promised herself an early finish which was customary every Friday in Rome.

Trevor Miles left his comfortable home and drove back to London, parking in the underground car park which ran all the way under the stockbroker's office of Martin and Jackson. He took the lift to the sixth floor and acknowledged the greetings of the staff. He ignored the coffee offered by one of the girls and continued to the back of the office where he lifted a small flap covering the thumb print entry to the rooms behind. Placing his thumb on the screen, he was immediately admitted.

'Hi there,' came the response from his boss, Paul Jansen,

who had just poured himself a black coffee. 'Do you fancy a strong coffee? You look like you might just need one.' He grinned. 'We'd best get started; we have many items to discuss this morning.' Trevor accepted the offer of the coffee and settled down in the chair opposite his boss, Paul Jansen, the UK's chief of M15.

Tom Rendell opened his eyes and, for a brief moment, wondered where he was. He certainly felt relaxed; in fact, if he was honest, he felt physically drained. His thoughts quickly returned to the evening before and, as he lay there in the large, comfortable bed, he reflected on the events that had started with his tie being seductively removed and quickly followed by the remainder of his clothes. Good grief – the lady had uttered no more than a dozen words and he had ended up in her bed! That was, of course, after the leisurely sexual romp on the white fur rug in front of the roaring fire. Lady! The Lionel Ritchie song 'Three Times a Lady' would never have quite the same connotations for him again. The woman was insatiable: after the first time on the rug, as he recalled, the next had been around two in the morning, followed again at five, when he found parts of his body being caressed and this exquisite form positioning herself on top of him and literally performing what could only be described as a rape of his person. Tom grinned to himself; it would, however, be rather foolish for him to take the idea of rape any further!

    Getting out of bed, Tom was amazed to see his leather overnight case, last seen in his hotel room, sitting on the small table in front of him. His surprise continued as his gaze fell on the suit he had worn the previous evening; it had obviously been pressed and was hanging up along with his recently laundered white shirt. He entered the en suite bathroom and was immediately impressed by its opulence. It was designed with 'his and hers' in mind, the thoughtfully chosen colour scheme indicating straightaway the side to use according to your gender. Each had its own special basin and mirror with cleverly concealed lighting. The central feature of the bathroom was a double shower cubicle, obviously designed for both parties to use solely or together. The overall splendour of it all made his bathroom at home pale into insignificance.

Tom used his own shaving gear and then showered vigorously, as if to remove all signs of his sexual encounter the night before. Past experiences of this kind had taught him to ensure that no traces of perfume or lipstick could be detected by any third person, most particularly Trish, devoted secretary and lover. Returning to the luxurious bedroom, he put on his newly laundered clothes and was surprised to find a set of diamond cufflinks. He wondered briefly, as he pushed them into the appropriate slots in his shirt, if they were payment for services rendered.

Leaving the bedroom, he found his way to the top of the grand staircase he had climbed the evening before. If he could remember correctly, he had been led up there behind the slender, swaying bottom of his hostess, but his memory was a little blurred!

Tom found that the house had come alive with scurrying staff carrying out their duties; one of them standing at the bottom of the stairs motioned to him to enter the breakfast room. He found his hostess already sitting at the end of a long table, sipping her coffee. Even at that time in the morning, he noted that Connie's appearance was in every way inch perfect. Her white silk housecoat was as closely fitting as her dress had been the night before. Connie looked up at him with a polite smile. 'Oh, good morning, Mr Rendell, please sit down and join me for some breakfast.'

Tom, rather taken aback by this formal greeting, did as he was bid and within seconds was presented with a printed menu. It offered a selection of breakfast food which he knew he would certainly not have been privileged to enjoy at the bed and breakfast lodge where he had originally chosen to spend the night. He selected a croissant with jam preserve, leaving the butter on the silver tray. He actually did consider having some eggs, bacon and kidneys, having acquired a considerable appetite from somewhere. However, he could tell from Connie's manner that she intended this to be what Americans love to call a 'breakfast business meeting', and did not want to delay in hearing his hostess's requirements. Aside from which, he knew he would soon be getting a phone call from Trish asking how things had gone the evening before and whether he had obtained the instruction.

Madame Connie Pasteur waited patiently until Tom had finished his croissant and coffee and, as if not wishing to prolong the suspense any longer, she got up from the breakfast table and, with a sweep of her slender hand, beckoned the hapless estate agent to follow her. Feeling somewhat relieved when she walked past the grand staircase, Tom followed her through two large polished oak doors which led into a library. His hostess went to the end of the room as if she was going to retrieve a book from one of the many shelves. Stopping, she placed her hand on a particular book and seemed to push. With that, the section gave way to reveal a hidden room that lit up as the façade swung open.

Tom entered the room and was amazed at the number of paintings lining the walls; he estimated at least thirty, maybe more. Connie remained silent as, speechless, he walked around the room taking everything in. He thought he recognised the work of several Grand Masters and stopped in awe when he found himself looking at a very good copy of the Mona Lisa.

Connie came up to where Tom was standing and he was again conscious of her perfume which seemed to engulf him. She guided him as she walked slowly back to the entrance of the room, indicating as she went the works of many well-known artists, the names many of whom Tom recognised, others he did not. Closing the door behind them, she led the way back to the drawing room they had occupied the evening before. The fire in the grand fireplace warmed the room making the intoxicating presence of Connie Pasteur even more prominent than before. Tom shook his head; he was finding it extremely hard to listen to his hostess without recalling the passion of the previous night.

She came straight to the point. 'Mr Rendell, I would like you to dispose of all the paintings that you have seen in that room – do you think you can do that?'

Tom's mouth dropped open. 'Pardon, Connie – err, Madame Pasteur!' he exclaimed. His jaw dropped as he sought to make sense of this latest revelation from his hostess; what on earth was she saying? Surely she must have meant the château!

Connie repeated her request and stood watching him, an expectant look on her face; she clearly required a direct answer and she required it now.

Tom found himself spluttering that he was actually an estate agent and not an art dealer. Surely, there had to be a mistake. Trish must have misheard Madame Pasteur's instruction.

'No, there is no mistake, Mr Rendell. I think you would do a good job.' By now Connie had sat down on the large white sofa and was indicating for Tom to join her. 'I will explain: when my husband died he of course left everything to me: the house, the grounds and, unfortunately, some considerable debts. He also left me directions on how to locate the room we have just been in along with details of each painting, the expected worth of each and the estimated value of the entire collection.'

Astounded, Tom asked, 'But the house, do you not wish to dispose of the house?'

'Heavens, no,' Connie replied with a look of amazement, almost as if he had asked her to give the house to him. 'I don't wish to sell the château. Whatever next?'

Dropping all sense of this being a business meeting, Tom sighed. He was out of his depth here and knew it. 'The thing is, Connie, while I have enjoyed myself – err... your hospitality, greatly, I am not an art dealer and would not know where to start.'

Connie smiled, as if for the first time acknowledging that something had taken place the evening before. 'You should not worry about that, Tom; my husband gave full instructions where the paintings should be offered and to whom. I did, in fact, try an art dealer in New York, but I was not overly impressed and he has made no progress to date, which is why I contacted your office.'

'A proper art dealer would handle the sale of these copies much better than I would and get you a much better price,' Tom persisted.

Connie raised her eyebrows, her face lighting up with surprise. 'Mr Rendell, the pictures are not copies – they are all originals!' She looked blankly at Tom's shocked expression. 'Yes, including the Mona Lisa!'

Chapter Three

Jessica Banks put down the phone after her weekly call from Cassie, bringing her up to speed on where their boss was spending his time. He had in the past made some surprise visits to keep them on their toes but, for the last two years, this practice had been discarded as if to show that he did indeed trust his remaining staff. The fact that he was in France gave Jessica the chance to take a few hours off to buy a few items from her favourite lingerie store. Tom always complimented her on her nightwear before he yanked it off. It had been well over four weeks since his last visit and she was missing him. The liaison was not to her liking but Trish was in a more commanding role than she and had been for the last five years, so Jessica made do with the little time her boss gave her. For Trish's benefit, they went through the pretence of booking him into the local hotel only for him to ruffle up the pillows and come creeping back to her room. The one time she had stayed in Tom's room they had almost been found out when an early morning call from Trish was put through. Jessica had answered but, quickly realising the mistake, had pretended to be the chambermaid and, in a performance worthy of an Oscar, had said that Monsieur had already gone down to breakfast.

In London, Trevor Miles was pouring himself another black coffee.

'So what's up?' he queried, sipping the hot liquid.

'Do you know Luke Sanders in New York?' Paul asked him.

Trevor nodded. 'What about him?'

'He called a few days ago to ask if we knew of anyone who was selling Old Masters in France. He only asked, he said, because according to his contact the painting that was being offered around for sale was apparently already hanging in a New York art gallery!'

'A copy – most likely.' Trevor shrugged. 'So what?'

'Not really, Trevor – the man doing the offering was a well-known dealer who insisted the picture was one hundred per cent genuine and the one in the museum was the fake. If it had been anyone else doing the offering, Luke said, his contact would have laughed in the dealer's face. What is more, the dealer indicated that there were more where that one came from.'

Trevor eyed his superior. 'Well, this is all very interesting, Paul, but not really what we'd call "in the interest of National Security".' He grinned.

'I'm inclined to agree with you, but we should perhaps keep our eyes and ears open, wouldn't you say?'

Trevor laughed. 'I wouldn't have it any other way! Now, what else is new? It's so quiet out there I am getting to believe that all the spies have gone home for an early Christmas or something.'

Tom looked at the serious face of Connie Pasteur as if he was observing her for the first time. He noticed that, beneath her immaculate make-up, a few tired lines were emerging and he wondered how he had missed them the night before; after all, she must be in her early forties, perhaps even slightly older than himself. He realised he had been only too willing to be seduced in every sense of the word by her exquisite figure and presence; the delightful scene of flickering candles, the blazing warmth of the fire, the outline of her figure... He stopped there; his mind was wandering again. He tried to concentrate on the subject in hand, but knew it was not going to be easy.

Bringing his thoughts to bear, Tom decided he needed more information. Why had Connie approached his office at all when she must have known he was, indeed, an estate agent? Smiling across at her, he put the question.

'Well, to tell you the truth it was only after reading your book *Would you buy a house from this man?* that I chose you.'

'My book!' exclaimed Tom. 'But I wrote that at least five years ago.'

'Maybe, but I remembered reading it.' Connie shot him a mischievous smile, adding, 'And your picture did you proud.'

Tom laughed out loud, recalling that the cover photo had shown him much younger than he was now and had been a deliberately provocative pose to make the best of his smouldering good looks. It could explain Connie's insistence that he came last night – the little minx! 'Really, Connie,' he spluttered, 'it's not worth us going any further with this. I am not an art dealer and my forte really is selling houses.'

Connie pursed her lips, a slight flush suffusing her cheeks. 'What is your average commission for selling a property of say – around a million euros?'

He thought for a moment. 'We might get two per cent in England – over here, somewhat more. Why?'

'If I tell you I am willing to pay you ten per cent for each sale and the overall value of the pictures in my gallery is well over two hundred million euros – would that be of interest to you, Tom?'

Tom caught his breath, his eyes widening. 'Did you say two hundred million euros?'

'Yes indeed,' came the reply.

His mind whirling, he tried to make some sense of the incredible figures the deal conjured up. His business had always ticked over and he enjoyed a good lifestyle. His staff still managed to cover the costs of his two offices and only last week he had been feeling smug that he had the world at his fingertips – not to mention the many fringe benefits that were available to him, but what Connie was suggesting would put his income in a new light and, if he could sell just two paintings, he could almost double his pension fund overnight plus...

Tom was suddenly conscious that his hostess was looking enquiringly at him, expecting an answer. Attempting to hide his elation, he leaned forward. 'You make an offer that is hard to refuse – so I guess we have a deal, Madame Pasteur.'

Connie's smile broadened. 'In that case, Mr Rendell, we must shake on it.' Taking Tom's hand, she pulled him towards her and, standing, led him back up the stairs.

The text that Trish received was short and sweet: *Everything is fine, deal is exceptionally good, call you later with full details! xxx Tom*

Trish smiled to herself; love him, he must have put a lot of effort into this deal to even mention it as 'exceptional' because she knew Tom was never one to enthuse too much about any deal. Yes, she thought, a lot of effort must have been put in to get it sewn up so quickly. I'll be extra nice to him when he returns.

Chapter Four

As Tom drove back towards the Channel Tunnel, he repeated over and over again in his mind the tale that Connie had finally confided to him after they had finished 'shaking hands' on the deal. It had taken most of the afternoon to accomplish this and Tom knew he would have to use the tunnel, rather than the ferry, to make up for lost time. He had planned a golf meeting with a friend in Windsor; he would have to reschedule that.

Evidently, Connie's husband Boris had been the son of a German Count and just before his father's death he had been given the secret of the art room, as it was called. It transpired that the Count had been close friends with a top-level SS officer in the last war and, when asked to look after some items of great value, had agreed. One night well after dark, a German army lorry had turned up unannounced and left several wooden crates which Boris's father had readily stored for his friend. This happened many more times over the next few weeks and then nothing – no further word came to the château. Several months later, the Count learned that his friend had been killed when the staff car carrying him and two other officers had been strafed by an English Spitfire. They apparently had been on their way to see him.

It was only upon examining the boxes that Boris's father had found the paintings and realised their true value. It also occurred to him that it was more than likely all the paintings had been taken or stolen from Dutch and German Jews.

One thing was for sure: they were much too hot to handle at that time. However, over the next few years, one by one, his father had sold the odd painting through a close friend, hence the grand style in which the Count and latterly his son and daughter-in-law lived. Upon his father's passing, Connie's husband had managed to sell only one of the masterpieces and, not willing to expose himself to the more rigorous scrutiny of the present art world, had gone deeper and deeper into debt.

Tom's feeling of euphoria was coming to an end. This deal, although very lucrative, must have a certain level of danger, not to mention that it could be completely illegal and totally immoral, to say the least. By the time he entered the Channel Tunnel, he was having some serious second thoughts about his last forty-eight hours. He sat in his car, his mind in turmoil; what on earth was he supposed to do? He shook his head as he realised that just recalling his time with Madame Connie Pasteur was already giving him an erection.

It was late on Friday evening when Trevor returned to his Windsor home and was met with the usual display of love and affection from his wife and children. It had been an uneventful week; the foreign agents of the countries he normally had to keep an eye on must have retired or gone on holiday. He loved his job but was always conscious that he had to play the part of the stockbroker personified, even to his wife and children. He was pleased when Saturday morning came and he was able to get in his car and make his way to his local golf club for a well-earned game.

Tom Rendell made an excellent job of leaving his problems back in France and, upon arriving home, managed to play down his anxieties about his new instruction. He did not go into the full details of his trip, only explaining that the company would be handling some paintings that would yield a good return. After a night of lovemaking, Trish was only too pleased to accept anything her handsome boss had to tell her.

Trevor got up from his seat and welcomed his golfing partner. 'Glad to see you again, Tom. Did you have a good trip to France?'

'How did you know about that?' Tom asked, surprised.

'You need to ask? You know how the girls talk. Trish was moaning to Allison that you were away again. By the way, did you remember her birthday?'

Tom gave a look of exaggerated horror. 'Oh my God, I completely forgot – now I am in the soup – again.'

Trevor laughed. 'Never mind, if that's all you've got to worry about I guess you can cope with eating some humble pie.'

Huh, Tom thought to himself, Trevor was a nice guy, but he didn't know the half of it – did he?

Tom's and Trevor's families had been friends for several years after Tom had arranged the sale of the Windsor property that Trevor and Allison now owned. Tom, being a golfing addict, had introduced Trevor to the sport and even sponsored him at his golf club. It was just the thing for Trevor to get involved in; getting away and hitting a few balls helped to offset the demanding week at the offices of MI5. Not that Tom knew anything about Trevor's work; like everyone else, he thought Trevor was a successful stockbroker who worked away in London for most of the week. The girls had struck up a friendship despite Tom and Trish not having any children. Well, not yet anyway.

The two men chatted as they went around the course and, with Trevor gaining ground on Tom's handicap, they eventually called it a day, had a few drinks at the club bar and left. They knew they would be seeing each other in two weeks' time as Allison had invited Tom and Trish to one of the children's birthday party at the house.

After putting his concerns neatly behind him, Tom had arranged with Madame Pasteur for Jessica and Cassie to go to the château to catalogue the five paintings that would be offered for sale gradually over the coming months. He wanted to involve both of the girls because they each possessed a good knowledge of art, Jessica in particular, but he had agreed with Connie that they should know only about the first five to be sold. The paintings listed were to be presented as if they could be original masterpieces, but without actually stating that claim. In the art world there was bound to be someone willing to let his mind drift into overdrive; greed – as Tom knew only too well having succumbed to it himself in this instance – was always a good motivator. The selected paintings would be removed from their secret hideaway and placed on the walls of the château as if they had been there for many years, giving the impression that Madame Pasteur was simply selling off a few of her heirlooms. Only Tom would know the full truth.

Jessica and Cassie were pleased to have a break from their humdrum work schedule and enthusiastically made their plans to meet in Paris so they could drive up together to see the client.

Upon arrival at the château, they were greeted warmly by Madame Pasteur who immediately requested that they address her as Madame Connie to make things a little less formal. It was soon clear to Cassie that Jessica had taken an instant dislike to the Frenchwoman, but Cassie was taking her time in making up her mind. She admired the smooth aristocrat manner in which Madame Connie moved and the way in which she dressed. Yes, Cassie thought, as far as she was concerned the woman portrayed many of the traits that she herself would like to emulate. One thing was for sure: this Madame Pasteur was right up Tom Rendell's street. Cassie could readily understand exactly how the company had landed this lucrative contract; their boss would have done anything it took to get it.

Tom Rendell was now extremely busy travelling around Europe trying to make contact with some of the names on the documents that Madame Pasteur had given him. It was proving difficult; for one thing, half of the contacts had passed away, a few were in jail and the rest had moved away to destinations unknown. This was not going to be easy.

Increasingly disheartened, Tom finally arrived in Brussels in an effort to contact the last remaining name on the shortlist. He thought he would have some lunch first and then try to find this Mr Jonathan Green. After a quick bite, Tom finally found the address he was seeking, only to find out that Mr Green was out at a local tavern. Great, Tom thought, with my luck I guess he will be well drunk when I do find him. He entered the Green Dragon which to Tom sounded very English and asked around the bar for the mysterious Mr Green. Surprisingly he was directed straightaway to a man sitting at the end of the bar nursing a small beer.

Tom decided to make the approach as if he was a stranger in town and just making friends. As he approached, the man turned and looked intently at him; his eyes were a distinct green which seemed rather at odds with the dark black hair that cascaded onto his forehead. Tom was surprised to find that Mr Jonathan Green was, in fact, an American and was only too happy to talk with another English-speaking person, even if he was English! There was one small problem: he was not the Jonathan Green listed; he was his son, Jonathan Green Junior.

It did not take Tom long to discover that Jonathan Junior had taken over the family business after his father had passed away several years ago. In fact, Jonathan had been his junior partner for some time. Tom was impressed with this man's apparent knowledge of art and he decided to press on with his quest of selling the paintings. He would, of course, start with just one.

At Tom's request, they departed the Green Dragon to have dinner and enjoy their evening further.

At the château, Jessica, Cassie and Connie were getting on a little better after spending their first evening working on an in-depth presentation. This was made easier due to the fact that the old Count had done his homework on all the paintings in his possession. He had also provided sketchy details as to the areas from which the paintings were 'acquired'. After the war, it would have been relatively easy for some of the paintings to be reunited with their owners or, as in most of the cases, relatives of the murdered rightful owners, but Boris had never undertaken this task.

One thing was for sure, Madame Pasteur's relationship with Tom Rendell was much more than a strictly business one; Jessica was absolutely convinced of that. The glowing manner in which Connie referred to Tom showed that he had obviously made a big impact on the lady of the manor. Jessica had secretly given the main bedroom the once-over in a vain attempt to find something, anything, to prove that her boss had indeed mixed business with pleasure. It was perhaps this distraction that got in the way of Jessica's knowledge of art for she failed to recognise, or simply refused to believe, that the paintings were anything but good copies of Old Masters, and Connie did not enlighten her.

Madame Pasteur was herself equally certain that Jessica had more than a platonic relationship with Tom Rendell; she made a mental note to talk with her new business partner in order he might confirm that what she suspected was correct.

After completing their task, the girls were then asked by Madame Pasteur if they would mind carrying out an inventory of all her possessions with the view to seeing what else she could sell. Jessica however was increasingly aware of the constant references made by the lady of the house indicating that her brief time spent with Tom Rendell had been much more than a normal business meeting.

Cassie, for her part, could see they were circling each other like a couple of hens fighting over a cock and predicted it would not be long before the feathers started to fly; of that she had no doubt.

Tom Rendell was completely oblivious to all this as he poured his new found friend another glass of red wine.

Chapter Five

Trevor had been called into Paul Jansen's office. 'I'm sorry to call you in, Trevor, but we're again hearing things that puzzle us greatly, to say the least.'

Used to Paul overstating the facts, Trevor waited patiently for his boss to come to the point.

'It seems that someone is going around Europe trying to find the whereabouts of known art dealers of some repute – and others not so honest.'

Trevor looked directly at his boss. 'This may be so, but why are we bothered about some paintings doing the rounds? It's still not something that's exactly threatening to national security. If anything, it's a job for the police, surely?'

'Granted, but it's unusual for so many enquires about so many dealers at one go – clearly, someone has something big to sell and it's our job to observe and make note of things that strike us as unusual. I know you're probably right, Trevor, but,' Paul tapped the side of his nose, 'I've a feeling about these strange happenings in Europe. Where there's art there's lots of cash, and lots of cash could mean lots of drug money. It bears watching, OK? Make some discreet enquiries.'

'OK, Paul, you're the boss.' Trevor left the office and made his way to the coffee house on the corner where he knew he would find some Russian and French acquaintances having coffee – at least he would have some old mates to talk with.

*

Tom had played it clever, at least so he thought. He was making conversation with Jonathan about art and managed to slip in that he had a friend who was trying to sell a good copy of an old masterpiece. Jonathan was immediately interested; times had been rather lean over the past year with the recession hitting the expensive pursuits of some of the rich men of Europe. The problem Tom faced was: how could he convey to Jonathan that there was a distinct possibility of the painting in question being much more than just a copy? He started innocently enough. 'I was wondering, Jonathan, how do you guys tell what is genuine and what is not? I mean, to my untrained eye the painting in question looks completely genuine.' He paused 'Do you have any books on it?'

Then he sat back; he knew he had pandered to Jonathan's professional pride, sowing the seed, and he waited patiently for his new friend to come up with the expected answer. It was not long in coming.

'Books are of limited use. You have to have an expert look at them and I know just the man who could do it.' The jubilant Jonathan smirked. 'When can you get the painting so we can take a look at it?'

'I reckon I could get it within five days. Where does your man live?'

Jonathan's smile grew even wider as he said casually, 'Here in Brussels.'

The two men finished their meal, made their goodbyes and arranged to meet at the same restaurant in one week's time. Tom drove back to his hotel, pleased that he had at least made one contact to start things off.

Jonathan was equally pleased with his luck in finding a man who had what sounded like a desirable painting for sale. With times being slow – the availability and sale of good art pictures had been poor and he had a lot of bills to cover, not to mention a few gambling debts. It appeared that Tom was a nice enough man but, as with many 'nice' men, he was also a bit of a shmuck. Jonathan smiled to himself; he had a feeling he could make himself a packet with this one.

The news that Tom had made a good contact in Brussels was welcomed by Madame Pasteur who informed the two girls that they could relax for the evening before returning to their homes. It seemed that Madame Pasteur did not want them around when Tom Rendell returned from his trip the next day.

The next morning, Jessica and Cassie said their farewells and reluctantly left the château. Cassie felt a little disappointed at not seeing her handsome boss. He had always given her a warm welcome and seemed genuinely pleased to see her. Jessica, on the other hand, just felt evil towards Connie; her inbuilt alarm system crying out that her man was soon to be devoured by this extremely rich bitch. Neither girl gave their friend Trish any thought as they made their way back to their respective homes.

What was that saying? Desire conquers all!

Arriving some time later at the château, Tom was surprised to find that his staff had been sent home earlier than expected. He had assumed they would all have a meeting to review the work the two girls had carried out. He was forced to conclude however that it was for the best when, later that evening, he was ushered into the chambers of his new client who, with hardly any foreplay, proceeded to start from where she had left off just a week or so before. Tom was forced to admit to himself the next morning that it had been a lovely way to end an evening.

It was not long before he was making his plans to take

the picture, which was alleged to be a Guilo, and the new presentation documents to his meeting with Jonathan the following weekend. He was reviewing his schedule when his mobile rang: it was Jonathan. The venue had been moved because his 'friend', after learning of the subject of the painting, had decided that the best place to sell it would be in Rome. Could he please make his way there instead?

Tom readily agreed.

Chapter Six

Trish was not at all happy with all these diversions. She knew that Tom had to spend a lot of time in France and Belgium, but the recent visit by her two colleagues to the château had left her feeling a little bit left out. She also knew that someone had to mind the shop, but the thought of her lover being host to three extremely attractive women – for she had assumed from what little Tom had told her that the Frenchwoman was singularly attractive – had left her with a bad feeling in her gut. Her brief conversation on the telephone with Jessica that morning had confirmed her suspicion that the Countess was indeed not only very attractive but also extremely rich. It was not as though Jessica had actually admitted it, but she was not the only one with a built-in alarm system. It was with an anxious feeling that Trish went about her work that coming week.

Tom had left the Countess seemingly very happy with his efforts over the past week and, in particular, the weekend. A little jaded, he caught the flight to Rome after calling Cassie and asking her to book him a room at one of the best hotels. He felt good. He had been bedded and now, if all went to plan, he was on track to earn his first ten per cent of… his mind boggled at the number.

A short flight later, Tom stood patiently outside Rome airport, the carefully wrapped picture stowed securely in his overnight case. His face lit up as a red convertible pulled up and he recognised the features of Cassie. The car and its occupant seemed to fit in well with the glorious sunshine that Italy was enjoying at that time of year. Tom's gaze travelled eagerly over the young woman's form: her strapless dress revealing her tanned body, her smiling blue eyes, fair hair and tanned face, her red lips parting to show her beautiful, even white teeth.

'Hi, Tom, how are you?' she called gaily.

Tom suddenly realised just how much he always enjoyed his visits to the Rome office, even though he had never managed to get his office manager to come to dinner and... he managed to force the words from his mouth, 'Oh fine, Cassie, just fine.'

The afternoon sun continued to highlight Cassie's fair hair which glistened as she placed Tom's precious cargo in the boot of the car. His eyes were drawn to the outline of her body as she effortlessly pulled the boot lid down and got back into the driver's seat, her slender legs seeking out the correct position in order she could put the car in motion. His thoughts returned to previous occasions when in no uncertain manner Cassie had turned him down. What was the saying, he mused – the more you cannot have something, the more you want it? How true!

They exchanged small talk as they made their way from the airport. Cassie explained that she had booked Tom into a small hotel not actually located in Rome itself. He accepted her explanation that she had booked the room in this particular hotel mainly because of the privacy offered due to its secluded location. He nodded, noticing the wind catching Cassie's fair hair causing it to rise and fall onto her slender bare shoulders, and his eyes moved down her body to an even more delightful sight. His companion was wearing a flowing dress that fitted neatly in all the right places, but failed totally to conceal her deliciously firm, lightly tanned breasts. What was it about this young lady today? Tom could not work it out; she seemed different – almost as if she was 'teasing him'… surely not – he must be misreading the signals. Remembering the constant put-downs in the past when he had made his usual 'come to dinner' suggestions, Tom tried to put these poignant thoughts out of his mind. He began to wonder if at the best of times, when it came to the behaviour patterns of his female staff, he could sometimes be a little naïve.

He felt the soft wind stream over the moving car, seemingly trying to find a final place to settle but, failing to do so, shooting suddenly down around their feet. The effect of this was to cause the hem of Cassie's dress to flare and ride up her slender legs, exposing her inner thighs. Mesmerised, Tom could not concentrate on the small talk and found himself running out of words, his voice trailing off into unfinished sentences.

Cassie was intrigued. Her smooth, normally eloquent boss seemed to be rather confused today. He was not making any sense; his mind was obviously on something else. She reasoned that he must be missing Trish or perhaps even Jessica. Cassie did not give the Countess a second thought as she drove up the winding road that led to the cliff-edge hotel overlooking the lake. It was also fortunate that she could not read her boss's mind as she bent down to retrieve his overnight bag from the back seat, showing again two of her greatly admirable assets. She left Tom to retrieve his case from the boot while she checked him in at reception.

She led the way up to the room with its beautiful lakeside view that she had personally selected for her boss. Cassie was sure he would enjoy the room; after all, she had spent a nice weekend there with her ex-husband before it had all gone pear-shaped.

Tom's meeting had been arranged in Rome for the following

evening so he could relax tonight. He was pleasantly surprised when his request for Cassie to join him that evening for dinner was accepted. Good grief, that was a surprise indeed.

Chapter Seven

Jonathan Green made his way to meet his contact who had indicated he would be able to give a valuation of the painting for sale. He had arranged the meeting for the day before he was due to meet up with Tom as he wanted to check out the possibility of having two prices for the painting – one for Tom and another much higher for himself and the dealer.

Unfortunately, it was soon apparent that any appraisals given had to be genuine; Louis Diamond startled him when he announced that the client with whom they would be dealing would be the Vatican itself. It would be extremely inadvisable to try to deal with two sets of figures. Jonathan cursed silently, but resigned himself to play this one by the book; a bird in the hand…

Tom had finished showering and changed into some casual attire consisting of a short-sleeved shirt and chinos. He felt really pleased with himself; he was going to enjoy having dinner with a gorgeous girl. It would be nice to relax and talk, even if there certainly would be no big sexual conquest at the end of it, Tom thought, as he made his way down to the quaint little restaurant which looked out over the harbour with its fishing boats, all bobbing up and down gently in the dying swell from the nearby mountains surrounding the large lake. He did not have long to wait for his date. Cassie had done him proud. Her dress for the evening was simple but very alluring;

the short sleeves exposed her sunkissed arms, indicating to Tom that it was quite possible his brief glimpse of her tan earlier that day extended to every part of her shapely body. He welcomed her with a kiss on both cheeks, the usual practice in Europe. He had ordered a pre-dinner drink to include a favourite of Cassie's: a cocktail made out of special ingredients which, amongst other things, included passion fruit. Tom had also added a shot of vodka to the cocktail; if he was going to relax he wanted his date to do likewise.

Jessica and Trish had suddenly become firm friends, even more so than before. Trish had sensed that Jessica had not been completely straight with her when giving her the description of Madame Connie Pasteur.

Her phone call to Jessica confirmed her original conclusions that the Countess did indeed have many other attributes in addition to money.

Cassie, unaware that two of her colleagues were having a bad day, was enjoying herself. She stared intently at her boss's lean, handsome face, noticing every line. His smile seemed to get more endearing as the night progressed and, after the third cocktail, she was content to just sit there and admire the master of chat-up lines in action.

The appearance of a bottle of wine together with an excellent course of fish from the local lake completed the experience. Yes, Cassie was for once forgetting all her recent troubles with her ex-husband and finally putting it all behind her. That, of course, did not mean that she would go to bed with her charming boss; no, if they were going to have any future, Tom Rendell would have to prove himself worthy in every way.

Tom was also captivated by how things were going.

He glanced out of the window and noticed that the lights of the harbour seemed to complement everything that was unfolding before him. Cassie's smile seemed to convey to him that she also was enjoying the special evening. He noticed that her blue eyes had an unusual greeny hue, something he had not been able to observe before at such close proximity.

She finished her drink but refused another. She was already over the limit and would have to take a taxi back to her little house which she had occupied for the last six years. She enjoyed living on her own now, having been subjected to a rough kind of love by her ex-husband. Tom, very well oiled himself, knew instinctively that he at least should go through the motions of trying to get this lovely lady into his bedroom. He felt he had a reputation to uphold. However, he remembered then all those previous polite, but firm, refusals and suddenly he felt that he did not want to spoil the magic of this extremely enjoyable evening. He ordered the two of them coffee accompanied by two glasses of cognac; at least it would be a civil way to end the evening. As they clinked their brandy glasses, Cassie's eyes seemed to sparkle as she sipped just a small amount, her red lips moistening as her tongue savoured the flavour of the brandy.

God! Tom, looking across at Cassie, found his mind was in turmoil. What message was the lady was giving out? Was it green for go – or worse still, red for stop? For the first time in his life, he was at a complete loss as to what to do, but he knew it was time to make up his mind! He heard himself suggesting that perhaps they should conclude their very delightful evening. Cassie's face seemed to show a degree of disappointment, which only made Tom even more confused.

Cassie suddenly felt rather let down after all the previous innuendoes. It seemed that Tom was, at last, admitting defeat.

He might have at least given her the choice of saying no!

Tom stood up, swaying uncertainly on his feet. Gosh, how embarrassing. He had never been in the position that he could not handle his drink. Picking up his glass, he smiled sweetly at Cassie and walked unsteadily up the stairs leading to the bedrooms. He hoped he could find his key otherwise he would have to go back down to the reception and ask them to let him into his bedroom. He put his hand in his pocket and to his surprise pulled out the key. 'Oh, there you are – you little bugger!' How he had managed to climb the stairs was a mystery to him; he swayed along the corridor which led to his bedroom. He stopped at the door, pondered for a while and turned. 'I have forgotten something,' he muttered.

'Yes, me,' a stern voice said.

He felt the key being taken from his grasp and slowly leant back against the wall as a vision of loveliness opened the bedroom door for him. His colleague had come to his rescue and he found himself being gently ushered into the room and pushed backwards onto his bed. His consciousness dimmed, but he had the distinct feeling of being undressed. This cannot be happening again, he thought dazedly. Not twice in as many weeks. In the warmth of the Italian evening, his body felt no chill as he relaxed, moving obligingly only to conform with the gentle motions of some sweet-smelling person who now initiated the removal of his shirt and then his trousers. This surely was a lovely way to end an evening.

Tom found himself slipping into an extremely restful state, only to be brought to full consciousness as he felt the movement of a body rising and falling astride his prostrate form. He lay there enjoying the moment as a distinctly warm feeling seemed to engulf him. He opened his eyes and smiled. Good heavens, it was true: Cassie's tan did cover the whole of her lithe body. He moaned with pleasure and instinctively pulled Cassie down by her shapely buttocks, causing screams of delight echoing his own.

The movement of their two bodies intensified and soon they were engulfed in a frenzy of mutual pleasure, the heat and passion of the night causing them both to perspire profusely. Tom's responses were further heightened as sweat dropped from Cassie's pert breasts and slipped into his partly opened mouth.

As he fell asleep that night, exhausted from the evening's entertainment, he concluded that it was more than a match for the previous weeks. His thoughts were filled again with Lionel Ritchie's 'Three Times a Lady' – not again Cassie – not again!

Chapter Eight

Trish had awoken with a thick head; she had consumed a week's intake of white wine in one evening and was feeling the effects. Her imagination had run riot; she could only imagine that her boss Tom had most likely taken his countess with him to Rome, the eternal city of love, or was that Paris? She could not think straight. After showering and dressing, she went to the office wondering: should she phone her boss for an update? Doing something was better than doing nothing.

In comparison, Tom had awoken to a bright sunny morning and with a smug feeling. He had managed to 'tie one on' and, what was more, he had managed to put another notch on his headboard, so to speak. He reflected on the night before and concluded it had been a tough fight but, by golly, it had been worth the wait. He looked around and suddenly realised that his companion of the previous evening was missing. He got up, went into the en-suite bathroom and found Cassie drying herself off after getting out of the shower. He could smell her sweet fragrance from where he stood. He went over and put his arms around her; she turned around and landed him a sensuous, warm kiss.

Tom was half of a mind to guide her back to the bed but his thoughts were interrupted by the sound of his mobile breaking into its familiar ring. He looked at the screen and saw it was Trish, obviously wanting to have an update on the situation. He felt a little guilty; he could not really tell his secretary the truth, the whole truth and nothing but the truth.

'Trish, nice to hear from you,' he said breezily, indicating to Cassie to remain silent.

Cassie suddenly felt pleased; for the first time she was not on the outside looking in. She was the main player in an intrigue that went with having an affair with someone who already had, what you might call, a permanent commitment. She listened to Tom's lame excuses of having a quite early night etc, etc as she brushed her hair vigorously like she was brushing away some of her guilt. Guilt? Why should she feel guilty? She was a free agent and Tom, well, he was not actually married. Would she do it again? You're darned right she would!

Tom switched off his phone and shook his head. In for a penny, in for a pound. He led his sweet-smelling lady back to the crumpled bed. Breakfast would be a little late that morning – if at all!

Louis Diamond looked at the painting that lay before him in the suite at the Holiday Inn Hotel in Rome's piazza. His sudden feeling of inner excitement grew as his expert eye raced over the canvas; his sucking-in of air went unnoticed by the two men who stood back watching anxiously as the expert went about his task. Louis knew at once that he was looking at Giulio Romano: Mother and Child. His excitement grew even more as he pored over the canvas with his magnifying glass, looking at every detail and every stroke. As he went about his task, he was even more convinced that this was indeed a genuine Guilio Romano, one of the great artists of the fifteenth century. To the waiting men, it seemed to take an age, with the expert moving the painting to different parts of the room as if to get a better view of it in a different light. He stood up and gave his findings.

'This is very good, in fact excellent! I feel it must be a Giulio but I can't believe it as we all know where the original is. I think the only thing we can do is to go to the Vatican and see how they react to it. After all, there cannot be two of these pictures – or can there?'

Jonathan shook his head in wonderment but was surprised when he saw Tom's reaction; it was almost as if he had expected such comments.

Louis pranced around the room feeling as if he had won the Lotto? The Lotto? He felt he had won the European Lottery's first prize. He had to make plans for an audience with his contact in the Vatican and that could take several days. It was one thing having an appointment but, having seen the painting, he now had to convince the cardinal that his time would not be wasted. Meanwhile, it was agreed that Tom lodged the painting in the safe deposit at a local bank.

After doing this, Tom made his way back to his hotel. Upon his arrival, the receptionist called him over and explained that he had let Tom's secretary into his room in order she could rest up while awaiting his return. Tom eagerly mounted the stairs two at a time; he suddenly felt that even now, after such an eventful day, he wanted to recreate with Cassie the charisma of the night before.

Entering the room, he was greeted by the ample charms not of Cassie in Rome but his live-in lover and secretary from London. Trish was lying there naked, arms outstretched, waiting to be serviced by her handsome boss.

Evidently she had been to the Rome office and obtained the hotel's location from the ever-obliging Cassie, bless her. Tom knew instinctively that his run of good luck had now been badly compromised. He also knew that, despite it being a normal sunny day in Rome, storm clouds would soon be gathering.

It was alright to have secrets as long as they remained so, Tom thought ruefully while attempting to look pleased and surprised. His bedding of Cassie could now produce its own sort of problems.

His heart was not in it as he drew Trish to him in a vain attempt to hold his end up.

Chapter Nine

Louis Diamond entered the inner sanctum of the Cardinal's office and sat down. Cardinal Spencer looked at him sternly. 'Louis, it is only because of our long relationship that I have agreed to see you. Your comments have bothered me greatly and I am of the opinion that you must surely have taken to the brandy bottle one too many times.'

Louis returned the Cardinal's stare with one of his own. 'Your Eminence, I am convinced that the picture I have recently seen is genuine. It is not a fake!'

'You must be mistaken. We have the original in our vaults – of that there can be no doubt.'

Frowning, Louis was adamant. 'No, Your Eminence, I must beg to disagree.' He went on to argue the point, his stubborn attitude overlooked only because of the Cardinal's long-standing respect for Louis's expertise. In the past, Louis had assisted the Cardinal in the acquisition of many excellent works of art.

The two men, realising that nothing more could be accomplished by arguing, agreed the only solution was to bring the painting in question to the Vatican for a closer examination. A further meeting was arranged at noon the following day.

Tom, Jonathan and Louis entered the Cardinal's grand office promptly at noon and laid the painting on the desk, which was situated in front of a large window. Adjacent to the space allocated for the picture lay another picture, similar in size but covered with a cloth.

The Cardinal had gathered with him three of his own experts who immediately took over the examination of the newly arrived painting. They took their time, performing even more intensive tests than Louis had carried out. Then they turned their attention to the painting that had been covered. Long pauses were accompanied by quiet exchanges of thoughts amongst the three of them. Finally, they stood and nodded to each other as if they had reached a conclusion.

Cardinal Spencer looked expectantly at them. 'Well? What is your verdict?'

'We cannot explain it, Your Eminence, but we feel that this painting is a genuine Giulio Romano and could well be the original.'

'How can that be when we already have the original here on the desk?' the Cardinal protested.

'Well, Your Eminence, if what you say is true then one is a fake!'

A second expert went on, 'If that is so, it will take further examinations to find out which is genuine and which is not.'

Tom, frustrated, could not contain himself. 'Could there not be two?' he asked.

Chastised by the looks of horror that came from all the men gathered in the room, Tom lapsed into an awkward silence.

Moments later, Tom and Jonathan found themselves being ushered out of the Cardinal's presence as if they were now surplus to requirements. They only had to wait for ten minutes before Louis came out and informed them the sale of the picture had been agreed and the amount of ten million euros would be credited to an account of their choosing. There were no conditions to the sale and no discussion on the price; that was that. Thank you and goodbye!

The two men were shown out of one of the many side doors of the Vatican. They both walked silently as if they had been struck dumb. Suddenly, Jonathan let out a whoop of joy soon matched by Tom's and they waltzed around the large piazza as if they were at one of the many weddings that occurred there all year round.

Tom's agreement with Jonathan was straightforward: they would split the commission sixty-forty, payment being made to a Swiss bank account of their choosing after Tom's mystery owner had received 'his or her' full payment.

Tom returned to his hotel and immediately asked Trish to organise a 'bit of a do' at a local restaurant which was renowned for its excellent cuisine. Trish confirmed the booking at eight that evening. Cassie would be there by seven thirty for pre-dinner drinks. Tom wondered briefly how he would handle the coming together of his two mistresses; he knew very well from past experience that body language was responsible for many a giveaway. It might be easier if he brought someone else into the mix. He took out his phone and called Jonathan.

Jonathan Green ended the call with a smile of satisfaction. He pushed his dark hair back from his brow and stood up, stretching his six foot form. Yes, he would be only too pleased to accept this invitation to a celebration dinner. For one, he knew Tom would be paying but, more importantly, there was a good chance his new friend had other lucrative contacts in the art world; ones that he, Jonathan, might assist him with. Thoughtfully, he loosened his tie, checked his watch and switched on his laptop.

Chapter Ten

Tom glanced up as a taxi dropped two young women outside the restaurant. He gasped as he recognised the familiar forms of Trish and Cassie; each seemed to have attempted to outdo the other and he did not know who to look at first. Trish was wearing what looked like a newly purchased full-length red gown that showed all her attributes. Cassie was even more alluring in a peach silk dress that rivalled last night's gown for its close fitting.

They each planted a lingering kiss on Tom's cheek; then both sat down at the table, one on either side of him. As he welcomed both ladies, Tom felt strange; was it that his recent sexual experience with Cassie had had a different effect on him than he first thought? Was it possible that Tom Rendell, sexual predator extraordinaire, had lost his heart?

The arrival of Jonathan made no impression on either Trish or Cassie; they simply nodded their acknowledgement of his presence then immediately returned their attention to the man at the centre of their affections.

Taking the only available seat directly opposite Tom, Jonathan soon realised that he had next to nothing chance of getting even to first base with either of these two gorgeous girls. Of one thing he was sure: his rival held all the cards and was playing them close to his chest. What was obviously Tom's was going to stay Tom's – well, at least for that particular evening. He shot an amused glance across the table, sensing that the estate agent was not entirely comfortable with the situation.

Trish, observing Cassie's body language, began to sense all was not well. She picked up straight away on the chemistry that seemed to be emanating between her boss and Cassie and knew that something had happened between them; there was no way the two had remained 'just friends'. Her heart sank as Tom turned his attention almost entirely to the other woman. Any hope of Trish retaining the sole interest of her boss was disappearing almost as quickly as the wine being served with the meal. Cassie, with all the experience of five years of marriage, had obviously out-foxed her within the last forty-eight hours.

Clearly, Trish realised, her Italian colleague was not as naive as she appeared. Looking at the scene unfolding in front of her very eyes and taking into consideration the half-hearted effort Tom had made upon her unexpected arrival in Rome, Trish could only conclude that the cards were indeed stacked against her. Tom had given up any pretence that everything was normal between them, and Cassie, for her part, appeared not to be worried if her long-time friend and colleague knew or not.

Trish sat there wondering what her next move should be. Having lost her appetite, she picked at her prawn starter and did even less damage to the main course of lemon chicken. As she tried to no avail to get and hold Tom's attention, she began to realise that her time with her boss had come to an end. Refusing a dessert, Trish decided she should now try a different approach; she was a woman scorned and did not intend taking it lying down.

Jonathan was surprised when halfway through the dessert he felt a definite stroke on his leg. Having given up all hope of ever enjoying an intense discussion with either girl, he could not believe his luck. He knew it was not Cassie; wrong direction and Tom was miles away. It had to be the delectable Trish. He turned to the now apparently very much available lady and gave her all his attention.

Trish looked at Jonathan with new interest; he was quite good-looking with a good strong physique and, from what she could see, he was obviously interested in taking their 'chat' further. Finally, she excused herself from the table only to return five minutes later with a key in her hand. Taking Jonathan by his hand, she looked calmly at Tom's rather surprised face and said, 'Well, Jonathan and I are off now then. Goodnight.' With that she and her new man exited the scene. Her expression said it all: a new queen was in town – long live the queen.

Chapter Eleven

Jonathan had really enjoyed his night. He had eaten an excellent meal at no cost and then he had received more attention than he had bargained for. He had been on the receiving end of the amorous actions of a female who seemed to have something to prove to him – or perhaps to herself. Jonathan had managed to keep his end up but, by golly, this woman had almost brought him to his knees. He smiled as he looked at her sleeping form beside him. This couldn't be true, a first-time meeting culminating in a sexual romp that had left him spent. What is more, he would soon have four hundred thousand euros in the bank, which would help take the heat off from the people to whom he owed money. Life was looking up!

Trish opened her eyes and realised what she had done. She left the rumpled bed and went into the bathroom without a thought for the man with whom she had just spent an extremely eventful night. Tears fell down her face as she looked in the mirror and noticed that the night's activities had left their mark. Women of her age should get at least eight hours each night – she had hardly managed two! She wiped her face and returned to the bedroom, ignoring the expectant look from Jonathan who had now regained his breath, not to mention his libido. Turning on her heel, she headed back to the bathroom, showered and dressed. There was another problem: she would look completely out of place going down to breakfast dressed as if she had just come from the opera, so she called room service and ordered breakfast for herself and Jonathan.

Upon its arrival, Jonathan attempted some small talk, mainly geared to finding out if he would be fortunate enough to see his lady of the night again. However, in the midst of their chat, he discovered something of even more interest. It appeared that Tom Rendell had four more equally desirable paintings at his disposal. Now that certainly was of very real interest to an art dealer who happened to be in desperate times!

Tom and Cassie had returned to the hotel somewhat relieved that they could freely conduct their love affair in the open. Trish's acceptance of the situation, by leading Jonathan off for a night of passion, clearly showed that she had at least resigned herself to the revised set-up. Tom was just getting around to thinking that the problem of sorting out their living arrangements would have to wait until he and Trish were both back in the UK when his mobile rang. It was Jonathan, asking if they could have a meeting that day. Tom agreed and they arranged to meet at the café near the Vatican in St Peter's Square.

Tom arrived on time to find the art dealer was already sitting there with a cup of coffee and a pleased look on his face.

'Hi there,' Jonathan hailed him. 'Would you like a coffee? How do you take it, black?'

'Hi. Yes, black will be fine.'

Jonathan came straight to the point. 'I understand from Trish that you have four further paintings to dispose of. Is that correct?'

Tom, inwardly cursing Trish for letting the cat out of the bag before he was ready, had no option but to confirm that this was indeed correct. 'I will have to confirm that the owner still wishes to proceed with the sale, though,' he cautioned.

'When will you know? I feel that, if they're of the same

calibre, the Vatican will most likely be interested in them as well.'

'I'll be in contact with them today so I'll let you know tomorrow,' Tom replied, not wanting to be rushed, 'but I do know that it would be only one painting at a time.'

Agreeing to talk again within the next two days, the two men parted company and Tom left to return to his hotel and make his phone call to Connie. He could see that the latest development in his love life might just complicate things, but he had no option other than to return to the château to see Connie so they could select another painting. A further goodbye with Cassie was almost as strenuous as the last and Tom was glad to have the respite of a few days' travelling in order to regain his composure and strength. Tom Rendell was suddenly feeling his age and, while recent events had been extremely pleasurable, he did have a job to do. He also had to face Trish who would not be in a good mood by any stretch of the imagination. First though, he had to stop off in Paris to set up the next sale and, from his experiences of Madame Pasteur to date, he knew that this also would not be without some further strenuous effort from himself.

Arriving at the château, Tom found that his client was in an extremely good mood. Connie insisted that a celebration was in order and the treat would be on her. She had booked a table at one of the local restaurants and ordered her car to be brought around to the front of the house. The evening went well and Tom was pleased that she was happy with the price paid for her painting. She indicated that she thought he had driven a hard bargain and that she would have expected only around the six million mark. Tom decided that he would not enlighten her that the price had been set on a 'take it or leave it' basis by the Vatican itself. Still, one had to play the game to one's best ability and perhaps he might not be so fortunate next time with the price. He had a chance to observe again her features close up and he noticed that, when compared with his Cassie, the Frenchwoman came out second, although her figure was exceptional.

The evening concluded with Connie leading the way to the bedroom and Tom, of course, was expected to perform to his usual standard. He was amazed at his own stamina and the gasps emanating from the Countess confirmed that the stud had not lost his touch. The next morning, he managed to get to the bathroom first so that he didn't have to give a repeat performance and he headed for the breakfast room even before Connie had showered. If she had any misgivings about this, she did not show it as she joined him at breakfast. Tom muttered that he was starving despite the large meal they had shared the evening before.

After they finished breakfast, Connie and Tom went to choose the next painting to be sold. They chose a Van Gogh and, after it was duly packaged, Tom made his farewells and left to return to Rome.

He had decided against going back to Windsor at that time. He realised that Trish now had another string to her bow and suspected that, by exposing his interest in Cassie, he may have also confirmed his fling with Connie, for where there is smoke there could well be fire. Tom realised that he must be slipping and there might come a time when he would have to choose between the women in his life.

Tom's return to Rome was welcomed by Cassie and she straightaway invited him to her home for a cooked meal. This was followed by the christening of Cassie's bed and Tom was relieved that the new lady in his life seemed content with just the one performance. His desire to bed her had landed him with a problem: too much fun and not enough devotion to work had left him exhausted, and he reckoned he should do better in future and concentrate more on work.

Convening with Jonathan and Louis at the usual meeting place was straightforward enough with Louis again marvelling at the authenticity of the painting. He looked at Tom with a strange expression on his face. One picture similar to the accepted original could be explained, but two?

Tom shrugged his shoulders as if to say he was only the messenger, not the seller. He had not bargained for such an in-depth examination by Louis who seemed to have a lot of experience in Old Masters. Later, the same three Vatican experts as before scrutinised the picture with much nodding and muttering. Eventually they made their offer: eight million euros – take it or leave it. Tom was totting up numbers in his head, a little surprised and mightily relieved that the possibility of wrongdoing with someone replacing the originals with copies seemed not to have occurred to any of them.

Chapter Twelve

Tom and Jonathan left the Vatican wondering if they had lost their touch; the Van Gogh must surely be worth at least as much as the Giulio Romano. On the other hand, they were only too pleased that, once again, they had disposed of a painting with such ease. Neither man had any real idea of its true value.

Tom, uncomfortably aware that he had some ends to tie up in Windsor, made an excuse to Jonathan and left Rome without a further visit to Cassie. He was sure she would understand that her man had things to sort out with Trish and, as far as Cassie was concerned, the sooner that was done the happier she would feel.

The news was out: Trish had arrived back in Windsor and put the word about to anyone who would listen. The first to hear that Cassie was now the one and only object of Tom's affections was Jessica who had to hide her annoyance from Trish. As they spoke on the phone, she looked at the new, unused nightwear she had purchased several weeks ago and bit her lip. She could not figure out where it left her; knowing that Cassie of all people had deposed of Trish in one fell swoop. Did it mean she was now out of the pecking order completely or would she remain in her usual second spot as before? She did not believe that her flirtatious boss could ever stay true to one girl at a time; he would surely expect the same favours when he visited her again. Jessica resigned herself to the fact that she would just have to wait and see how things worked out. She knew Tom would most likely need to have his fill of Cassie before he returned to his old ways.

Trevor and Allison Miles had received the news with mixed feelings. Allison, of course, was incensed that her friend of many years had been dumped. Trevor wondered how his friend managed it. He had never met Cassie but had seen photographs and remembered her as being quite nice looking. However, he decided to refrain from saying too much about what had taken place between Trish and Tom.

Tom's arrival at the family home was tainted from the start. Both he and Trish had openly been 'at it' with someone else, but it did not make the situation any easier.

Trish knew her feelings for Tom were as strong as ever, even with the newly accepted knowledge that his dalliances had been not just with Cassie, although that was bad enough. Her accusations that he had performed with Madame Connie (as the French rich bitch liked to be called) had been met with a shrug of his shoulders as if to say, 'A man's got to do what a man's got to do!' That reaction had ended any possibility of an immediate reconciliation. Trish responded by asking, 'Well, Tom, who is staying and who is leaving?'

'Of course, the house will be yours,' Tom said instantly. 'I'll move out as soon as I've found another place to stay.' In the meantime, he thought ruefully: it's spare room time!

Cassie had received an irate phone call from Jessica, who basically accused her of betraying her; not even bothering to mention the betrayal of poor Trish.

'It just happened,' Cassie excused herself, omitting to mention that Tom's ruse of getting her drunk had failed, resulting only in him becoming the worse for wear, enabling her to take the key from his unsteady hand and strip off all his clothes. The initial wanton use of Tom's body was, of course, nothing to do with Jessica. Things just happen and… well, all is fair in love and war.

Cassie then asked the question, 'Will this affect our friendship, Jessica?' The sudden slamming down of the phone left her in no doubt that future relationships between her and Jessica might just be a little uncertain. As for her friendly chats with Trish, well, she guessed that they also must be in some doubt.

Tom struck his golf ball hard, just managing it to get to the green. Trevor laughed. 'I guess your stamina has taken a beating over the past few weeks, Tom?'

Tom smirked at his grinning friend. 'You don't know the half of it, Trevor.'

'Do you mean there's more?'

Mistaking Trevor's question to mean was another woman involved, Tom laughed and proceeded to relate his time at the château with Madame Pasteur.

Shaking his head in disbelief, Trevor listened in amazement. Never, ever, had he been confronted by a lovely woman trying to tempt him into betraying his marriage vows – chance would have been a fine thing. He smiled to himself.

Tom, of course, didn't know of Trevor's real job and, if he did, he would doubtless imagine he had been seducing all those female Russian spies much as James Bond did in all his movies. The truth of the matter was quite different: Trevor Miles, licensed to kill, had never been in a position to boast about saving the world by accommodating a female secret agent; more's the pity. Trevor loved his wife and family but hey, come on – get thee behind me Satan – but please, let the ladies show themselves briefly to me before you do! Keeping these thoughts to himself, Trevor swung his club and landed the ball within feet of the hole.

A few weeks later, Tom had settled into his new flat close to Windsor Castle when he received two telephone calls: one from Cassie enquiring how he was coping with his domestic changes and the other from Connie who was wondering if he would like to go over and spend a long weekend with her at the château.

This was the first time that Madame Connie had revealed that she was now as much interested in Tom as for his selling the paintings for her. It would seem he had done an excellent job of selling his own kind of art to the sophisticated Frenchwoman. Tom was now faced with a dilemma. Where did his true affections lie? Were they going to be spread between Cassie, Jessica and Connie or should he ditch his new life and return to Trish, if, of course, she would have him back. He knew that his new business partner, Jonathan, had been sniffing around her again. Trish had left signs at the office that clearly indicated she now had a new man in her life. Tom was not yet certain how he felt about that.

Trish, attempting to settle into a life that did not include Tom, had to admit to herself that Jonathan, if she was truthful, did not ring all her bells. Well, at least not like Tom Rendell. What she needed was a real man in her life who would stop her thinking of her ex-lover. That was easier said than done. She knew that she would eventually have to find other employment; she enjoyed working in the estate agency but Tom had made it impossible for her to stay – damn the man.

Tom made excuses to Connie, blaming the move into his new flat and his trying to get everything straight. He did, however, make a trip to Rome to spend time with Cassie. He found her less complicated than the other women in his life, and she had scaled down her demands in the bedroom. He started to relax and enjoy just being in Rome. Yes, things were much more settled since he had attached his wagon to Cassie's, but how long this would last was anyone's guess.

Madame Pasteur was not at all pleased when a few days later she called Tom's office and learned from Trish that, although he had told her he was busy moving into his new flat, he was in fact now in Rome with that woman Cassie. Not used to being given the brush-off, Connie saw red. The fact that her estate agent-cum-art agent had netted her around fourteen million euros was of little significance as far as she was concerned.

Tom was summoned back to France to visit his client who now wanted to put more pictures up for sale. He was informed that he would be required to sell three of the remaining paintings in order they could move on to the jewel in the crown: the Mona Lisa. Tom was worried when he heard Connie's plans to put the three paintings on the market simultaneously. He rang Jonathan who greeted the news with great enthusiasm. He would contact Louis and arrange a meeting to view all three paintings at the same time.

Arrangements were made for one week later, at the usual place. Accordingly, Tom made his way to collect the paintings. He entered the château with some apprehension sensing that Connie may have at her disposal further information about his dalliance with Cassie or even Jessica. He realised that he had compromised his position with her by entering into a sexual relationship and he knew he could only blame himself and no one else for that. He was pleasantly surprised, therefore, when Connie behaved in her usual manner, wining and dining him and, of course, leading him to her bed. Her eagerness to continue from where they had left off a few weeks ago was apparent. She forced herself on him almost hourly. Tom realised that he had a nymphomaniac on his hands and that his partner was certainly making up for lost time. He lay there panting for breath while she appeared to slip into a deep sleep. Thank God for small mercies, he thought. He could at last recover some of the spent energy.

He crept out of bed and made his way downstairs to the kitchen to see if he could get himself a cold drink. He had just finished a cool glass of milk when he found he was the object of a skilfully thrown bread roll, soon followed by another. Tom looked around and found a scowling Connie, her eyes blazing and her hand reaching for another object – a wine glass which, he instinctively knew, could cause him some serious injury if it found its target. Her first instinct had been to bed him but afterwards, when she pondered on it, she lost her temper at the thought of Tom having slept with someone else. After all, she now considered him a partner in more than one sense.

He didn't bother to ask her why she was acting this way and, rushing towards the irate female, attempted to hold down her flailing arms which sought desperately to release the latest object. Connie's eyes streamed with tears as she fought like a tiger in an attempt to hurt this man who, in her eyes, had betrayed her. Tom somehow found the strength to restrain her as she was now struggling like a wildcat. He pushed her against the side of the kitchen table forcing her back until she was almost completely off the ground, taking the sting out of her attack and pushing himself on top of her in an attempt to hold and calm her down.

The choice of words coming from the irate lady showed her extreme disdain for him and their being uttered in French was disconcerting to say the least. Tom had only one option: he forced himself between her flailing legs, closing his mouth on hers in a vain attempt to silence the obscenities that cascaded from her lips. If this continued, it would bring some of the servants running. He wondered briefly if her anger would stretch to her naming him as a rapist. Suddenly, her demeanour changed and he found himself being tightly held by Connie, a hand grabbing him tightly between his legs. He suddenly found himself sexually aroused and, as if by magic, Connie's short nightdress parted to reveal her breasts and hardened nipples. As he entered her, he was conscious of peace and quiet for the first time since he had drunk his cold milk. However, the silence did not last long: crockery, glasses and cutlery were pushed off the table and sent crashing to the ground as the couple sought to find more space in order that they could reach the ultimate peak of their desire. Tom finally pulled himself away from the prostrate Connie, his energy levels completely depleted. He could not continue; he was shattered. As he pulled himself together, he became aware that he was bleeding profusely and realised that his lover had inflicted one more assault on him by biting his mouth. Had it been in the height of passion or was it, maybe, in revenge? Tom knew he would not bother to ask her to explain. He had heard of 'Angry Sex' – but this was ridiculous. And how the hell would he hide the wounds from Cassie?

    He stumbled back to the master bedroom and wondered if he would be the object of more abuse. He was not to find out. Falling across the bed exhausted, he dropped instantly asleep.

    Waking up next morning he found Connie's arm stretched protectively over his body as if to say, 'Well, that's all right then!'

Chapter Thirteen

Tom left the château with the three paintings securely stowed in the boot of his car. Before he drove away, Connie planted a kiss on his cheek and he realised that he had managed to defuse a situation that could have threatened the very essence of this money-making opportunity. Perhaps she was informing him that 'angry sex' with her outweighed normal sex with anyone else. Tom was totally confused as he made his way to Rome where he would try to sell three more paintings and, of course, he would have to face the charms of the new lady in his life: Cassie. He licked his wounded lips and wondered if she would fall for the story that he had cut himself shaving. Fingers crossed!

Of the two, he was bound to conclude that the first task would be much easier than the second. Meeting up with Jonathan and Louis, he was soon to be met with disappointment however. According to Louis, the Vatican were not interested at this time in any further paintings until they had satisfied themselves as to the authenticity of the two they had already purchased. After dropping his bombshell and almost as if he was agreeing with the logic of the situation, Louis left.

The two men sat in silence trying to work out their next step. Here they were in the middle of Rome with three potentially very valuable paintings and nowhere to go. Jonathan was the first to speak.

'I think I might know someone else who might be interested,

but it will take a couple of days to set up the meeting.'

Tom nodded. 'We don't have any choice, do we? I do feel a little exposed hanging around here with these valuable paintings.'

The two men parted company, Jonathan going off to make his plans to contact the potential buyer and Tom taking the paintings to the bank's vault before returning to Cassie.

Within twenty-four hours, Jonathan was back on the phone. Yes, his contact was very interested and they could meet a week from today.

'Why so long?' Tom asked and was greatly surprised by Jonathan's reply.

'Well, the man has to come from Moscow.'

It transpired he was one of the richest men in New Russia, having made his money in oil. No, Jonathan told him, he did not own any football clubs; just oil and plenty of it.

Back in Windsor, Trish was feeling rather blue; she was getting used to not having Tom in her life and, while she was still being paid by the company, she found that her heart was not in it. Sitting in the lounge at home was not her idea of life in the fast lane. At least with Tom she had been able to travel about regularly and meet new people. Since her trip to Rome, she had hardly set foot outside the front door. It was then that she received a phone call from Jonathan. His invitation to join him in Rome that weekend sounded like just what she needed; it would be a nice change. 'No, you won't be bumping into Tom,' remarked Jonathan, as if to reassure her that no uncomfortable meetings would occur.

'Fine,' she replied, already reaching for her small case and putting in some of her prettier things. She might even put in her latest item of seductive nightwear. No reason to waste it.

At the hotel, Trish was warmly greeted by Jonathan who had pulled out all the stops to make the new lady in his life feel welcome. Sitting in the restaurant where they had first met did not have the same connotations as before. Trish had moved on and she for one wanted to put everything behind her. She would give her new man a chance.

Jonathan was now really attentive and he picked up her mobile phone to take a picture so she could show all her friends that she did have someone who cared for her.

The night's lovemaking was vigorous and extremely satisfying. Jonathan's suggestion that they go for a drive the following day was even more inviting. It dawned on Trish that, even with Tom, she had not really toured the surrounding areas that included the picturesque vineyards of Tuscany. In the car she stretched out her long legs and, with a contented sigh, leaned back in the seat, her face lighting up in a broad grin as she felt the warmth of the sun through her flimsy top. God, but it was good to be out! The further they drove through the lovely countryside, the more relaxed she became, the tension of the last few weeks falling away and becoming a distant memory. From time to time, she glanced surreptitiously at the man beside her who, unlike Tom, seemed eager to ensure she was enjoying herself. It dawned on her that in fact Cassie might have done her a favour.

She reached over and placed her hand on Jonathan's leg, gently massaging the inner side of his thigh.

He smiled. 'Not now, Trish, I'm driving, but keep that thought!'

Chapter Fourteen

Tom collected the paintings from the bank vault and placed them in his car. He would park the car somewhere safe until he had checked out the new potential buyer. Arriving at the café, he waited in vain for his partner to arrive with his Russian friend. He was glad he had left the paintings in his car; his mind started playing tricks with him and he had a funny feeling in his gut that he could not explain. He knew his choices were limited, but if things did not work out this time there would surely be plenty of other opportunities to make a sale. After all, paintings these days were money in the bank and people were happy to own even good copies.

Time passed and Tom finally gave up. He left the café, returned to his car, then drove to the bank to deposit his precious cargo. He then made his way back to Cassie; perhaps she would have heard from Jonathan.

She was sitting in her lounge reading a newspaper. She looked up, surprised that Tom had returned so soon. She had imagined he would call her to announce the successful sale of the paintings. No, she had not heard from Jonathan, but invited Tom to sit down and have some food. She liked having her lover at home with her; it was almost liked being married again.

She had not been fooled by the story of how he had cut himself shaving. Cassie recognised the marks of angry sex when she saw them, but she was a realist and knew Tom fancied himself as a stud. She reasoned that, if she chose not to rock the boat, his infatuation with Madame Connie would eventually fade, and so she had pretended to be taken in and smiled to herself at his obvious relief. Men were so easy to read.

Jessica was finding things quiet; her boss had not contacted her since his visit to Paris to arrange the sale of the pictures. Their business had ground to a halt. It had been hard enough last year with the recession, but now it was even worse. In the past, Tom had generated a lot of their income when he had visited her but, since he had been tied up with the sale of the paintings, things had certainly dropped off. Presumably the client would eventually kick through with Tom's commission. Jessica hoped so – for all their sakes.

Trish and Jonathan were having a great time. They had visited many places of interest, including the Leaning Tower of Pisa, and Jonathan had been busy with his camera taking numerous pictures of both Trish and himself. Trish laughed as he acted the goat, pretending to fall off the wall and disappearing from sight, only to pop up further down. This was a side of him that she had not seen before. The more she spent time with him, the more she started to have strong feelings for him. Jonathan never mentioned Tom and she never asked, not even how the sale of the paintings was going. Tom Rendell's name was taboo. Jonathan had booked a hotel room for several nights in order they could spend as much time together in comfort. Yes, Trish could get used to this.

Tom had given up trying to contact Jonathan on his mobile phone. It seemed the dealer had vanished off the face of the earth. He thought he had better return to the UK so he could contact Connie from a safe distance. Also, Tom felt he should perhaps check on Trish for, while he had now accepted she had finished with him, they had spent many years living as man and wife. He would call on her and see how she was coping – perhaps take her out to lunch or dinner. The thought of seeing her again suddenly rekindled some of the old desires he had originally felt for her.

Tom arrived at Trish's house but, after several attempts pushing the doorbell earnestly, he gave up and made his way to meet up with Trevor and Allison.

His arrival at their house was met with a cool response from Allison but a much warmer one from Trevor who was only too pleased to hear what his friend had been up to for the last few weeks. He and Tom left the house to get away from the stony silence that Allison still maintained when Tom was around. A friend indeed to Trish, but it did nothing for close harmony in the Mileses household. There was only one place to escape: the golf course – and the freedom that gave the two men, albeit for different reasons, was immense.

Trish and her lover had taken an early lunch. They were relaxing in a log cabin booked by Jonathan as part of his weekend treat. Weekend! This was now their fourth day and it was turning out to be more like a proper holiday. Trish wondered if she should contact home to see if any messages were waiting for her. However she decided against it; if any were there they could wait. She had other priorities on her mind that afternoon and redoubled her efforts to repay her new man for his welcome treat. Afterwards, Jonathan handed her a cup of coffee and announced apologetically that he had to contact Tom to arrange another sale possibility and she should relax until he returned. Trish smiled; she liked being pampered. She lay back and relaxed as ordered.

Observing that Tom was not hitting his handicap by any means, Trevor started thinking they should call it a day. If he could beat Tom this easily then something must be wrong. They retired to the clubhouse for a leisurely lunch and a few drinks, Tom bringing his golfing partner up to date with his love life and how he had managed clear the table at the château with Connie, much to Trevor's amusement. It seemed his friend was living a life that Trevor for one, could only read about in the Sunday newspapers.

The sound of Tom's mobile interrupted his tale just as it was coming to a very interesting part. Trevor let him answer; he could wait.

Tom looked at the screen of his mobile which showed Trish's number with a multimedia attachment. Funny, he thought, puzzled. I wonder what she is sending me at this time. He opened it up and gave a gasp of dismay. Was this some sort of joke?

'Anything wrong?' Trevor asked, seeing Tom's troubled expression.

'I'm not sure.' Tom handed him the phone.

Looking at it, Trevor was amazed to see a figure which he immediately recognised as Trish, lying on a bed. She was partly clothed and appeared unconscious. The next moment, a text came in with a short message: *If you wish to see this woman alive again you will leave the three pictures at a place to be advised. Failing this, you will never see her again.*

Tom gazed white-faced at Trevor. Neither of them could believe what they were reading – it didn't seem possible. After all Trish had been out with Allison just two short weeks ago. Where on earth could she be now?

Trevor had many questions to ask his friend. 'What's happening, Tom? What pictures are they are talking about? And where was this photo taken? Do you recognise it?'

Tom shook his head, his shoulders sagging, and he looked helplessly at Trevor. 'Well, err, I've been trying to sell some old paintings for Madame Pasteur, not her house as I led you to believe. I have two partners helping me: a man called Jonathan Green and an art expert called Louis Diamond. We managed to sell two – to the Vatican of all places! I went over recently taking three more paintings that Madame Pasteur wanted to dispose of. The thing is – '

'Look, Tom,' Trevor interrupted, 'never mind that now. You have to go to the police and tell them what's happening.'

'I'm not sure I can. Whoever has Trish must surely be watching me and will know if I do. I can't risk it, Trevor.'

With one look at Tom's troubled face, Trevor suggested that they return straightaway to Tom's apartment. It would not be a good idea to alarm Allison and the children. Tom agreed and the two men rapidly left the clubhouse.

Chapter Fifteen

Trish woke up to find herself lying on the bed in a strange position. For some reason, she could not move. A small light was on at the bedside, but her eyes would not focus properly. With blurred vision, the room swirled around in front of her.

There was no sign of Jonathan. Her eyelids began to close; she felt extremely tired and needed to rest. Her thoughts dimmed as she slipped into unconsciousness again.

The next morning, Trevor, looking as worried as he felt, hurried into the office of his boss, Paul Jansen.

Paul took one look at his face and said tersely, 'What's up?'

It took only minutes for Trevor to brief his boss on what had happened over the weekend.

'Let me get this straight. You're saying that your friend, Tom Rendell, is mixed up in selling stolen paintings to the Vatican and that his secretary has been kidnapped? Why come to me? It's a matter for the police, surely?'

'Tom dare not go to the police. He's afraid for Trish. Besides, he didn't say the paintings were stolen. In fact they appear to be legitimately owned by his client. The thing is, Paul, if you remember, you were worried about reports of someone selling Old Masters in Europe. Surely this has to have some connection?' Trevor fidgeted with the car keys in his pocket; not for the first time, it occurred to him that his boss was a bit slow.

'You're right, of course.' Paul nodded thoughtfully. 'Well, if you can't get Rendell to go to the police, we will have to assist him without his knowledge, but I don't want you jeopardising your cover, even if he is a good friend. Get in touch with one of our operatives in Rome, arrange some accommodation and then check it all out. I suggest you tell Allison you have to attend a string of business meetings in Europe so you can move about without raising any concerns from her. OK?'

'Yes, sir,' Trevor said wryly, wondering if his boss would ever stop telling him how to do his job.

Tom sat on his bed and gazed at a picture of Trish taken in happier times. He had repeatedly tried her mobile but getting no reply. His thoughts were broken by his phone beeping for attention. It was Jonathan, ringing to apologise for the delay in setting up the meeting. He had been forced to go Russia, he explained, hence the delay, but the contact he had made was already on his way to Rome. All that was needed now was for Tom to deliver the paintings so the dealer could evaluate them.

Tom listened distractedly, his thoughts with Trish. Where the hell was she? What was he to do? His pride stopped him from asking Jonathan if he knew where Trish was at that moment. Much as he wanted to ask for Jonathan's help, he did not feel it appropriate over the telephone to tell him what had taken place. He said he would meet him in the usual place as originally planned. He caught the next available flight out to Italy and within hours was making his way to the café.

Jonathan arrived on time and sat down with a smile. Yes, things were going well; the Russian contact was an extremely wealthy man and welcomed the chance to invest some of his wealth in art. His smile turned to a grimace of horror as Tom showed him the picture of Trish on his phone.

'It can't be right!' Jonathan exclaimed. 'I was with Trish only a couple of days ago. She came over for a weekend visit. Err, you know, of course, that we've been seeing each other, Tom...' he added almost apologetically.

Tom nodded. 'Yes, I do know, Jonathan, but – '

'We must do as they ask,' Jonathan interrupted. 'We can't put Trish's life in danger.'

'I agree, but don't forget the pictures are not ours to give.'

'But what does that matter? There's a life at stake here. The pictures are insured – aren't they?'

'Well no, they're not.'

'I can't believe they're not. Why not?'

'It's complicated. And anyway, you can't insure pictures that may be original. The premiums would be unaffordable – even if there was an insurance company willing to take it on.'

'Don't be silly, Tom, I know they are really good copies but they are surely just that.' Jonathan laughed out loud.

'Then why do you think the Vatican has a problem with buying or even looking at these pictures? Louis and the experts in the Vatican must believe that they might be original or have been painted by well-known contemporaries.'

Jonathan's laughter quickly died. He frowned, as if he could not understand what Tom was telling him, but Tom could sense that Jonathan's mind were racing. If this was true, these paintings were worth even more than the large sums they had been offered.

'Well, Tom,' Jonathan said after a moment, 'whether they are copies or not, I still feel we have to trade the pictures for Trish. After all I do feel responsible for her now, having spent all these weeks being with her, taking care of her – since you dumped her.'

*

Trevor had arrived in Rome and spent the day having meetings with his associates in the local office. The information he had gleaned was useful: the man called Louis Diamond was indeed a respectable art dealer, well known for his excellent contacts in the Vatican. Jonathan Green was not so well thought of and was known to be fond of gambling. He had pulled off a couple of dodgy deals that had drawn the attention of the local police – not to mention the tax authorities. Other than that, he had not been in jail and seemed to be trading on his late father's good name. It appeared Green frequented a café near to St Peter's Square, using it as a meeting place. A few days ago he'd been spotted with a youngish red-haired woman from London on his arm.

Armed with this information and receiving confirmation that Tom Rendell had flown into Rome that morning, Trevor came to the conclusion that he would have to do something he would normally never dream of doing: he would have to spy on his friend. Making his way cautiously to the café near to the Vatican, Trevor was pleased when he saw Tom was there talking to a man who, from the pictures given to him by his local office, Trevor identified as Jonathan Green. The two men were in deep discussion and Trevor could see from Tom's face that his friend was deeply concerned about what Green was saying. After a few moments, Tom seemed to nod his agreement and they both got up from their seats walking off in the direction of the adjacent car park.

Trevor was good at his job; he had spent years observing people who were involved in criminal activity and the one thing he did have was an abundance of patience. He had no problem identifying the two men as they left the car park in Tom's car, and he had no difficulty in following them.

After stopping at the bank to collect the paintings, Tom and Jonathan sped away from the town centre.

Trish was coming to. One moment she was aware of her surroundings, the next she had slipped back into unconsciousness. Gradually, the periods of awareness lengthened. There was no sign of Jonathan. When she did come to her senses, her brain could not function properly. She tried desperately to come to terms with what was happening to her. It was like a dream that was quickly becoming a nightmare. She could not move and she was very thirsty. Tears prickled under her eyelids and rolled down her taut face. Where was Jonathan; had something happened to him? He must have been struck down with the same sickness; yes, that must be it – she had sleeping sickness.

Tom and Jonathan made their way to a small village that had been specified in the latest text which Tom had received that morning. The village had one main street lined on either side with cottages. It would not have been difficult for someone to observe them without being seen. The instruction was for them to go to the post office and ask for a package, which they duly did. The postal worker gave them the small parcel after Tom showed him the necessary identification. It appeared that the kidnapper was taking no chances.

Inside were two things: a large lock of hair, which Tom immediately recognised as being the same colour as Trish's, even down to its three highlights. Whoever had removed the hair certainly had not skimped with the use of the scissors. The other item was a set of typed instructions that were simple to follow. They had to drive to a wood outside the town, leave the three paintings by a certain marked tree, walk one hundred metres further into the wood and there they would find Trish in a wood cabin. If they did not first leave the pictures, the person holding her would quickly dispose of her. It looked as if there were at least two people involved in this kidnap.

The two men did as they were bid, locating the tree in a clearing and placing the parcel of three paintings beneath it. They walked further into the wood, but found nothing – no cabin – no sign of Trish.

'This is ridiculous,' Jonathan said, after they had searched for several minutes. 'We have to split up or we'll never find her. It'll be getting dark shortly and we could walk past the cabin and not even notice it in this dense woodland.'

Tom agreed and the two men separated, each going in a different direction.

Chapter Sixteen

Trish's head was clearing, but she felt as if she had a massive hangover and her mind was blank. The last thing she remembered clearly was having lunch with Jonathan. Her head cleared as she came fully awake and realised she was sprawled half-dressed on the bed. She struggled into a sitting position. The cabin smelt damp. As she shivered slightly, it suddenly felt rather alien to her. Panting with the effort, she eased herself off the bed and found she could just about stand up without any dizzy spells. Glancing around for her clothes, she saw her top and jeans screwed up on the floor. After putting them on, she hunted for her mobile finding it eventually under the bed. How did it get there? The battery was dead; she had no means whatever of communicating with the outside world. She rushed to the door but found it locked. Helplessly she rattled the handle. Trying to hold down her panic, she turned to the windows. They too were locked and there was no sign of a key. She peered out and could just see into the woodland beyond the cabin. Darkness was falling, blocking out the light. Trish banged in frustration on the glass, shouting out for someone – anyone – to come to her aid, but there was only silence. She was about to give up when she noticed the lock on one of the window latches was broken. If she could find something to lever it out of position she might just be able to squeeze through the narrow gap. She looked down at her full breasts; she had put on weight comfort eating after the break-up. Trish bit her lip, the thought of Tom bringing her to tears.

Her luck was in: she found the knife she had used to eat the pizza she and Jonathan had shared yesterday. Was it yesterday? She had no idea how long she had been there. And where was Jonathan? She hoped he was alright but, if so, why hadn't he come back and found her? He must be sick or injured, lying somewhere.

Pushing hard with the knife, she prised the catch open and the window was released. Exhaling with relief, she shoved it outwards. The gap was smaller than she had envisaged but, drawing in her breath, she managed somehow to squeeze herself through it, ripping her jeans in the process. When she got home she would have to go on that diet; that was for sure!

Trish, still feeling a little dizzy after all her effort, steadied herself, her hand resting for a moment against the outside of the cabin. There was no sign of Jonathan or the car they had arrived in; where was that man? Walking towards the fading light, a trick she had learnt all those years ago in the Girl Guides, she knew that she was heading west.

She stumbled in the darkness but, more by luck than judgement, avoided falling headlong as she pushed aside the dense bushes that had grown up without any apparent interference from man. If only she'd had prior knowledge of the woods she might have been able to establish her whereabouts. As it was, she had no idea where she was. Slowly, Trish was getting her full senses back, and she gave silent thanks for that. Suddenly the trees thinned and she came upon a clearing where she paused for several minutes as if to get her bearings. As she glanced desperately around her, a strange shape caught her eye. She could just make out what looked like a large package leaning against a tree. Curious, she moved towards it. Funny, she thought, reaching out to touch the wrapping; it felt like the frames of pictures or something like that. Why would anyone carry a parcel of pictures to such an obscure place? Was the owner still nearby? She held her breath, listening hard, but all she could hear were the trees rustling and the occasional haunting cry of an owl. Shivering, she was getting increasingly anxious about where she was. She didn't feel safe in these dark woods and desperately needed to find Jonathan – or anyone who would get her out of this nightmare. Her gaze returning to the mysterious package, and she suddenly felt compelled to lift it. It seemed the naturally thing to do, she would worry about who the real owner was when she found her way out of this dreadful forest.

Trish was by no means a slight person but, even so, she had difficulty in picking it up. It was bulky and quite heavy. Leaving the clearing, she struggled with her burden and stumbled on her way, desperate to find a safe place.

Tom continued searching the area for the cabin as directed. He walked in circles; he doubled back, went to the left and right, still trying to remain in the general direction the kidnappers had given him. He tried to phone Jonathan to see if he was having any luck but the phone was dead; most likely no signal in this dense undergrowth. He would complain when he got back to the UK; the obvious boast of worldwide coverage was certainly a figment of the supplier's imagination. He decided to return to the tree; perhaps Jonathan had also come to the same conclusion. Tom was surprised just how close the clearing was but his heart sank as he discovered that the package of pictures they had left had gone. The damn kidnappers were certainly not playing it straight – God, he thought, what if they never had any intention of releasing Trish? His mind was in a whirl as he again phoned Jonathan, relieved when, this time, his partner answered.

'Tom, where are you? I've been completely lost for the last ten minutes. There's no sign of any cabin as far as I can see.'

'Me too,' returned Tom. 'I'm back at the clearing – and guess what – the pictures have gone!'

'What?' Jonathan yelled down the phone. 'That's not possible; you must be mistaken.'

'I assure you I'm not.' Tom was surprised at his friend's reaction. It seemed a strange thing to say; after all, he would have discovered the same had he returned to the cleared ahead of himself. However, he dismissed it. Jonathan's anxiety about Trish was obviously getting the better of him.

Jonathan returned to the clearing and they both examined the area carefully in case the package had been hidden. No trace. Eventually they gave up and returned to the car. There was nothing else to do but go back to Rome.

Trish was completely lost; she was tired, her legs were scratched and bleeding, and now it had started raining. Good grief, she thought miserably, her romantic weekend was going from bad to worse. Moments later, her worst fears were realised when, with no warning, a hand was placed over her mouth and, before she had a chance to scream, a voice in her ear told her to keep quiet.

Trish went rigid, stifling the scream in her throat. Her assailant had spoken with sharp authority and, if he was going to kill her, she did not intend to hasten her end by screaming.

The man eased his hand from Trish's mouth, turned her round gently and whispered, 'Please don't worry, I'm not going to hurt you. I'm on your side – believe it or not.' The voice was soothing and Trish felt a little calmer. She could see that her assailant looked normal – that is, if you could possibly identify baddies from goodies just by looking at them. She found herself being led gently to an open path and, within minutes, observed some lights which she realised were torches held by other people. Her nightmare was over, thank God.

Two men came forward to relieve Trish of the bulky package she was, despite everything, still carrying. The man who had come to her rescue identified himself as Ben Henderson and showed Trish an official-looking pass which she recognised as British since it had the Queen's emblem stamped on it. She found her voice and told Ben her name then poured out full details of the experiences she had been through, right from the start of the trip with her boyfriend to her sudden loss of consciousness – which she could not explain – and her escape from the locked cabin. Her boyfriend, Jonathan, had also disappeared, she explained, pleading with Ben to arrange for a search party to find him.

Listening to her speaking excitedly, Ben placed his hand on her arm. 'It sounds to me as if you were drugged.'

Trish laughed. 'Who the heck would want to drug me? I have nothing of value – unless… has it got anything to do with that package I found in the woods, do you think? It feels like pictures or something like that.'

She watched as the men brought the package to Ben. He nodded and, without looking opening it, put it on the back seat of the car.

'You may be right, Trish,' he concluded quietly. 'We will have to see, but not here. Let's get you back to your hotel – you have certainly had a narrow escape.'

The party returned to the hotel. Trish went up to her room to refresh herself and change her clothes while Ben sat in the lobby and awaited her return. While she was gone, he keyed in a text to Trevor Miles confirming his position.

*

Trevor had only just managed to hide when he had heard the crashing and cursing of someone coming towards him through the dense bushes. He had gasped as he recognised Tom's secretary, Trish. He had remained where he was and watched her pick up the package under the tree and begin examining it. Backing off, he had spoken quietly on his radio to one of his colleagues who was positioned on the other side of the clearing. 'Ben, keep the woman quiet and get her out of there. The kidnappers may turn up at any moment.'

'OK, boss,' Ben replied quietly.

One thing was for sure: Trevor did not want to reveal his true identify at this time; not in the middle of some wood in the dark. That would have been a little too hard to explain.

Chapter Seventeen

Trish returned refreshed and was about to ask Ben more questions only to be ushered out of the hotel and into another waiting car. As soon as she was seated in the back, the car pulled away from the hotel and Trish's requests for the latest information as to what was happening was met only with silence from the two men in the car.

Tom and Jonathan arrived at Jonathan's hotel and Tom went to call Cassie. Calming her down, he assured her he was fine and would be seeing her later, but first he had to call the police and inform them of the missing paintings. He refrained from mentioning that Trish had disappeared; she might have turned up while they were running around in the woods.

Jonathan went up to his room, leaving Tom pondering over the events of the previous night. Tom was uneasy with the whole thing; heaven forbid that Trish was in danger. He was beginning to hope that the whole kidnapping thing was an elaborate hoax. The ease with which the crooks had collected the paintings and vanished into thin air made Tom think it had to be someone local. They certainly knew the woods and seemingly it had been easy for them to evade both himself and Jonathan as they blundered about in the heavy undergrowth. One thing puzzled him though: how the hell had they known about the paintings?

The next day Jonathan returned to the cabin and was dismayed to find that Trish was missing. He knew he would have to come up with a good reason for not going back to see her. It was also possible that by now she may have left the country and returned to the UK.

Trish, having recharged her mobile, was perturbed to find no waiting messages. Jonathan had not been found and had not contacted her.

The next day, Trevor waited until he was informed that Tom had returned to the hotel and then called him, just as a friend, to ask how things were going. He greeted the news that they had not found Trish and had lost the paintings with the usual condolences. 'Don't worry, Tom,' he reassured his anxious friend, 'I'm sure the police will find her.' As soon as he had finished the call, he arranged for Ben to release the news to both Tom and Jonathan that Trish had been found safe and well, along with the paintings.

Jonathan now had a problem: his plan to get his hands on the paintings had gone completely haywire. He wanted to call Trish and find out where she was, but how could he explain away the rather delicate detail that he had apparently abandoned her to her fate? Eventually he made the phone call and was relieved that Trish sounded overjoyed to hear that he was safe. He came up with the excuse that he had been taken ill while he was away from the cabin, losing consciousness and not waking up until this morning.

Trish was amazed. That was exactly what had happened to her; she too had fallen asleep and not woken up until next day. There had to be a medical reason why this had happened; perhaps it was something they had both eaten? Jonathan listened to the details of how she had been rescued; the fact that she had ended up with the paintings instead of him was something he could only shake his head at!

Tom decided to let Cassie know what had taken place and, while she had no reason to be too concerned, she was certainly pleased that her adversary was safe and well. Cassie was by now very much installed as Tom's number one lady, and it was a position that would take a lot of change before she relinquished it.

Chapter Eighteen

Trevor had asked Ben to place the pictures under lock and key at the local police station in Rome. They would be released to Tom, who would have the necessary documentation to collect them. It was agreed with Paul that Trevor should return to the UK. Tom also decided to return to the UK when he would inform Connie about what had happened – he certainly did not wish to go into too much detail, not wanting to admit that he had lost control of the situation.

Upon his return to his UK apartment, Tom called Connie to explain about the delay in selling the three paintings. His explanations were met with a response which indicated that Connie was more worried about her agent than the actual paintings themselves. When was he coming back over to France?

Tom excused himself saying that he had a few things to do before he could return. After all, he had to fill out forms which had to be sent to both the Italian and the English authorities. He also knew he had to make arrangements to collect the three paintings before someone started asking questions about the status of them. He also made the decision to contact Trish and find out how she was. He was surprised to learn that she was now staying with Trevor and Allison in order to recover from her ordeal. Well, there was safety in numbers, that was for sure!

Trish treated her boss with some degree of indifference;

after all he had dropped her and she now had other fish to fry. Tom, realising that he would not be too welcome at the Mileses house – what with Trish's and Allison's attitudes – accepted Trevor's suggestion that they should retreat to their favourite place – on the golf course. This, of course, gave Trevor an excellent opportunity to find out exactly what had transpired with Jonathan. Alarm bells had been ringing for him; something about all this just did not add up.

Tom called Jonathan to try to establish what the status was of the Russian if of course there was one. The way things were turning out, Tom was beginning to doubt just about everything and everyone. Jonathan in turn assured him that the Russian was actually in Rome. He would contact him and come back within twenty-four hours to arrange another meeting in a few days. Jonathan suggested that Tom relax and take some time to get his breath back. Tom agreed; he just wanted time to take stock of things and, as suggested, get his breath back.

Trish was pleased to receive a phone call from Jonathan who immediately gave her some rather distressing news. It concerned Tom Rendell and the commission they had received from the sale of the pictures to the Vatican. His friend Louis had informed him that they had indeed received a higher fee than Tom had actually paid him.

Trish was really surprised to hear this – her ex-boss had never ever behaved like that before – surely he must be mistaken. Jonathan insisted: No, Tom had lied to him. He omitted to tell Trish that he had been present the whole time the sale had occurred. Continuing with his tale of woe, he went into a more depressed state; he would have to return to the States and try to make up the shortfall. The idea of losing yet another man in her life filled Trish with horror. He must reconsider, she protested. There must be something else they could do.

Finishing their game of golf, Tom excused himself and returned to his apartment; he wanted to prepare for his next trip to Italy. He realised that he had been neglecting his own business. He called Jessica in Paris and was brought up-to-date with the business enquiries and said he would call in to see her when things got a little easier. He had to make arrangements to collect the pictures from the police in Rome, and then meet Jonathan and his new Russian contact.

Tom made his way to Rome via the Euro-tunnel, but when the train stopped in Paris he decided at the last minute to call in at the office there. His arrival was a complete surprise to Jessica; after all, he had said he would not be going to Paris for at least two weeks. Tom gave her a warm smile and started looking through the books. He cut short his appraisal of the enquiries saying that most of it could wait, announcing that, after he had taken her to lunch, he would be heading off to Rome as he had to collect the paintings from the police station. Realising immediately that that also meant seeing Cassie, Jessica again felt left out. After all, their arrangement had been extremely satisfactory to both of them for the last five years. Why change things now?

She announced that she would have to go home and collect a few personal things before their luncheon date. Tom agreed; he had plenty of time before the next connection to Rome.

'Have you been keeping out of mischief?' he light-heartedly asked her.

'Tom, if you're asking me if I've behaved myself since our last meeting, the answer unfortunately for me is yes!'

Tom realised at once that he had not bargained for his response. He looked at his secretary and straightaway remembered the reason why he always enjoyed his visits to Paris. It was plain to see that Jessica wore no bra; the cleavage of her ample breasts showed above her low-cut dress and, as she walked, her nipples stood out firmly against the flimsy material. As they entered Jessica's house, she announced she would not be long and went upstairs to her bedroom. Tom realised that he had only been in the house once before and that had only been to collect some papers. His thoughts were interrupted as he heard Jessica asking him to come upstairs. He ascended the stairs to find a spacious bedroom in the centre of which was an extremely large bed. Jessica had her back to him and was struggling with the dress zip which had apparently stuck. Would Tom be so kind?

Tom found it relatively easy; it seemed to travel freely – up or down! He was about to inform Jessica of this fact when she stepped forward causing him to unzip the dress even further. She was now completely naked.

Tom wondered briefly to himself, How the heck do Frenchwomen do that? His thoughts were cut short as Jessica turned around pulling him to her. He hesitated, raising his hands as if to pull away. This could not be right; after all his heart belonged to Cassie. He now had feelings only for her. However, Jessica was not having any nonsense; she had been waiting for this moment for some weeks and she was going to collect what she felt was due to her, whether her boss wanted to or not!

Jonathan sat in the café trying to come to terms with the failure of his latest stunt. He realised that he had been stupid; trying to use Trish as a possible kidnap victim had been too risky to say the least.

Now he had failed to get the paintings and he had no Russian to pretend to look at them. He rang Louis and asked where he was. It appeared that he was sitting in a café just around the corner. Jonathan walked the short distance to meet Louis who immediately indicated for him to join him at his table. 'I'm glad I ran into you – I was going to call you and Tom. I have been requested to take you and Tom to the Vatican to answer some questions about the two paintings you and Tom have sold them!'

'I don't understand, Louis, the paintings are extremely good copies; what can the Vatican be worried about?'

'No, Jonathan, as far as I understand it, the paintings that you and Tom sold them are not copies – they are originals. The ones in the Vatican are the copies! Of this, there can be no doubt!'

Chapter Nineteen

Tom's efforts to pull back from the advances of Jessica were proving to be next to useless; her mouth closed on his as she pushed him down on the spacious bed. He sank further into the soft contours; if he had a bad back, the softness of this mattress would not do it any good! He felt his resistance weakening by the second as his shirt was ripped apart exposing his hairy chest; a touch of the James Bond – well, not quite that bad! Oh my God, not more angry sex! When, oh when had he lost the hunter's instinct and become the hunted! Next, off came his trousers together with the wrenching off of his slip-on shoes. Tom had no time to think of Cassie or what he was doing; Jessica's hands were everywhere, pulling everything free from his jockey shorts. The next ten minutes to Tom Rendell were ecstasy as Jessica's warm mouth entombed his now stiff penis. He groaned and his mind pitched into all kinds of thoughts; suddenly images of all the women in his life were looking down on him, one after the other. First there was Connie, peering over the top of Jessica's shoulder apparently looking on with interest; then Trish, well, she looked extremely angry; and finally Cassie, who had tears in her eyes. Oh, how could you, Tom Rendell, how could you!

Jessica was enjoying her moment of domination and increased the pressure on her unfortunate but now completely willing victim. It was the turn of Tom's eyes to fill with tears as he found the pressure almost too much to bear. He was about to lose total control when suddenly his assailant released her hold and repositioned her body. There was no need for her to hold on as she moved up and down as if to restake her claim on her boss, and perhaps as if to show him what he would be missing if he even dreamt of dumping her!

If he had been able to read his Jessica's thoughts, however, nothing could be further from the truth!

Cassie was now getting worried. According to the last communication from Tom, he was on his way to Rome and had been expected to arrive two hours ago. Her phone calls to his mobile went unanswered; he had promised to come to her first and then contact Jonathan. Two more hours passed and Cassie came to the conclusion that the person who might know Tom's whereabouts was either Jessica – or maybe even Trish. Calls to Jessica's phone went unanswered and the only other option was for Cassie to call Trish.

Trish answered the phone, recognising the name and number of her colleague in Rome. 'Hullo, Cassie,' Trish answered sweetly 'How are you – are you keeping well? How's Tom?'

Cassie immediately recognised an insincere tone. How could she now ask Trish where Tom was?

Cassie made her excuses and cut the call short. Trish smiled to herself. Looked like Tom was playing away already! Two from three meant one left unaccounted for; that had to be Jessica. Nice one, Jessica!

Tom's entrapment continued for the next few hours making it impossible for him to continue on his journey to Rome. Wow, that had been good! He managed to walk to the bathroom and showered. He found that his secretary had just finished cooking his favourite – steak and chips. What do people say about the best way of getting to a man? – via his stomach. Tom suddenly felt like he was in a fairy tale; Hansel and Gretel and the wicked witch were feeding him up to make him... Well, whatever it was, Tom was enjoying his juicy steak.

The next morning, after some more intense lovemaking, Tom managed to catch the early morning train to Rome. Jessica just smiled knowingly as if to say 'Take that, you swine.' She had become the hunter which made her feel that, for one small moment, she had been the powerful one and that had felt good!

His Eminence arrived on time and promptly sat the two men down as if he was about to hear their confession. He simply asked, 'Do you still have the other three paintings?'

'Y-y-yes, the other three paintings were still for sale,' Jonathan stammered, 'and I can arrange for them to be brought to his Highness.'

As they left, Louis seemed unconcerned at this latest revelation and, after they had had a quick lunch, he and Jonathan parted company. Louis went to his office whilst Jonathan was still having trouble coming to the conclusion that he might just be in line for an unexpected payout. Wonders would never cease.

Tom arrived at the police station. His time on the train had been spent trying to come to terms with the events of the previous night. He now had apparently come to an arrangement with three of his ladies; excluding Trish, that meant he could possibly continue his old ways; if, that is, he could get over the hurdle of explaining to Cassie his absence over the last twenty-four hours. He could not understand that, while he had enjoyed immensely the sexual romp, he felt extremely guilty, something he had never ever experienced in his life before. Cassie was special to him, but a man's got to do what a man's got to do! Yes, that was right – surely Cassie should realize that!

'I am sorry, Monsieur, but the paintings are not here!'

'What do you mean – they're not here?'

'Not here,' repeated the police sergeant behind the desk.

'That is impossible – who collected them?'

The man looked at the receipt in his hand. 'Well, sir, you did!'

Chapter Twenty

Tom stared at the desk sergeant with a look of dismay. There had to be a mistake; he had only just arrived from Paris going immediately to the police station. Who could have collected them without his say-so?

There was great commotion at the police station as everything was checked and counterchecked. The sergeant at the desk explained he did not know Tom at all, so why should he not have believed the person who had collected the paintings – he must have had the correct paperwork! Was it not Tom's signature? Tom looked at it and had to agree – it certainly did look like his signature. Further light was thrown on the subject when another policeman came on the scene and calmly announced that the person who had actually collected the paintings was a woman! She had been accompanied by a man who had picked up the package and taken them and the lady to a waiting taxi!

'We are sorry, sir, but everything is in order as far as we are concerned.' Case closed.

Tom left the police station and wandered aimlessly around the piazza, finally sitting down at a restaurant table, deep in thought. He needed to work out who would have known about the pictures being in the police station in the first place. Who would have had access to his signature and have the nerve to carry it off?

He was about to call Jonathan when the phone rang.

It was Jonathan, clearly excited about something. 'Tom, they want to buy the other three paintings!'

Tom, his mind still elsewhere, replied, 'Who wants to buy what?'

'The Vatican,' replied Jonathan breathlessly. Tom just sat there holding the phone to his ear – he was speechless! He could not believe it – a possible eighteen million euros and he had lost the paintings. Oh my God, what on earth could he do now? What could he tell Connie? He realised that he had to come clean.

'Jonathan, I've got some disturbing news – someone has collected the paintings from the police station and they've disappeared.'

Jonathan's reply could be heard all around the piazza: 'They've done what!'

'Disappeared – someone collected them from the police station using documents that had my name on them – and a very good forgery of my signature!'

The next ten minutes were spent with Jonathan asking for more in-depth explanations and Tom replying that he could not add anything more!

The two men had to meet and it was arranged that they do so that same afternoon. Tom decided that he had better call Cassie and make his peace. He found that he had an excellent alibi which he used to its fullest: that when he arrived late last night, due to traffic, he was unable to access the police station and... The rest came out in a rush, which left Cassie confused to say the least, other than the startling fact that the pictures she knew Tom was trying to sell had vanished or been stolen. The outcome was the same – he no longer had them to sell!

Tom remained at the café table wondering what to do next. The fact that they had the chance to sell the paintings now was bad enough, but to lose them to some con artist was too much to bear.

'You look like you've lost a tenner and found a pound.' Tom recognized the voice. Looking up, he found himself gazing at the features of his friend Trevor. 'What on earth are you doing here?' His friend ignored this question, saying instead, 'You look like you've won the lottery but lost the ticket.'

'You might say that. The paintings that were left at the police station have disappeared – they've been collected by some woman who gave a forged document with my name on!'

'What, someone just walked into the police station and collected them on your behalf?'

Tom sensed some amusement in his friend's voice but let it go. 'Yes, that's just about it.'

The two friends sat in the afternoon sun in the middle of the piazza, discussing the possibilities as to where the pictures might have disappeared.

Having been advised by his Italian colleagues that the paintings had indeed been removed from the police station, Trevor decided to throw in some thoughts he had been toying with since his discussion with Tom back in Windsor. 'Tom, if you don't mind me saying so, that business with Trish getting kidnapped and the sudden recovery of the pictures – didn't that seem strange to you?'

'What do you mean? I can tell you we searched high and low for her after we left the pictures in the clearing and neither of us could find the cabin! From what I understand, Trish was in a very confused state when the police found her and she had obviously been drugged or something like that!'

Hitting himself on his forehead then, he uttered, 'Good grief, I'd completely forgotten that Ben told me that she was asking about her boyfriend – an American!' Trevor groaned to himself at last, the penny had dropped. How the heck could an intelligent man like Tom fail to recognise that Trish had been with someone – that person being Jonathan Green!

'We'll have to confront him about this,' remarked Tom.

'Perhaps we should wait and observe where Jonathan goes and who he visits,' Trevor offered gently. He had a few days to spare so he could stay over and help his friend recover the pictures.

'You would do that, Trevor? That would be great!'

Trevor nodded, not believing his luck that he could now accompany his friend without giving away his cover. As they had time to spare, Tom invited Trevor back to Cassie's to meet her and have some lunch.

Their arrival at Cassie's was met with warm affection from Cassie; she was aware of Tom and Trevor's long friendship and straightaway she felt she was now being introduced to his inner circle of friends which made her feel good. Trevor, for his part, was immediately struck by Cassie's beauty and he could see how his friend had been tempted. As much as he had accepted Trish, he was himself attracted to this extremely sexy person. Those green eyes could tempt the Pope! What was he thinking – he was getting as bad as Tom with his wandering eye! Best keep his thoughts pure, but it was a hard thing to do.

Cassie produced a typical Italian meal of cheeses and bread accompanied by fresh ham, eggs and a nice red wine. Trevor thought about how the other half live; his normal lunch would have been a ploughman's at the local public house. Still, here he was in Rome, spending some quality time with his friend, doing a job which he loved: trying to solve the riddle of the missing pictures! Nice one, he thought to himself.

Chapter Twenty-One

In a dilemma, Jonathan, his plan of obtaining the pictures for himself having blown up in his face, could not believe his luck. He now had a cast-iron sale which was imminent but no paintings to sell. Calls from Louis went unanswered as he fought for additional time allowing him to solve the whereabouts of the missing paintings!

He sat in an agitated state tearing up countless cardboard beer mats, as if in an attempt to take his anger out on something. He was about to call Louis to ask for more time when his phone rang and he saw that Trish was calling him. Jonathan pushed the answer button and breezily asked her how and where she was. Trish surprised him by informing him she was in Rome again; could they meet as soon as possible? Jonathan groaned. In one hour he was due to meet up with Tom to discuss the missing paintings and now Trish wanted to see him, most likely wanting a nice sexy afternoon.

Deciding to come clean with her, he explained briefly that he and Tom had problems with the paintings and they needed to meet to discuss them.

'Oh, don't bother with that, Jonathan. What I have for you is much more interesting,' replied Trish disdainfully.

Jonathan was tempted; perhaps some angry physical love might just help rid him of his present frustrations. But what was he thinking – for Christ's sake, the paintings were worth millions – Trish could easily be replaced by one of many ladies he knew. Trish, however, persisted and Jonathan found himself agreeing to a meet within the hour, but he had to contact Tom to put off their meeting by an additional two hours – in case he got lucky!

Replacing the phone in his pocket, Tom turned to Trevor. 'Jonathan has put back this afternoon's appointment by two hours. What do you think we should do, Trevor – should we try to find him?'

Before he could respond, Trevor's mobile rang and he excused himself – walking away from the table to take what obviously was a business call. Tom waited for a few minutes while his friend finished his call.

Walking back to the table, Trevor suggested, 'Perhaps we should try looking around the hotel to see if Jonathan's actually staying here. That will allow us to observe where he goes.' Ben's update as to where the elusive Jonathan was had been most opportune.

The two friends were about to round the corner where the hotel was located when Tom pulled them back. 'You're right, Trevor, he's just leaving the hotel – we can follow him.'

Trevor agreed. 'You lead the way Tom – you seem to have a knack for this.'

Tom smiled. 'Yes, I guess I do – I'm not just a pretty face with a big appetite for ladies,' he added smugly.

Trevor smiled to himself. He was enjoying the amateur theatricals which were unfolding before his very eyes. Yes, his friend might just get lucky and solve the problem of the missing pictures all on his own. Trevor knew that if he did not, his fellow G-men, as the Yanks used to say, certainly would. He knew that Ben and the others were in the area and waiting on his signal to move in. They had to be careful not to move too quickly or it might scare off the mob or, in this case, most likely the Russian Mafia.

Jonathan walked nonchalantly from the hotel. If he had something to hide, the man was certainly playing it cool. He made no attempt to cover his tracks, finally sitting down at a table and ordering a coffee. Then he sat back as if to enjoy the afternoon sunshine.

The waiting men observed from a safe distance. Tom suddenly gasped as he recognised the familiar sway of a person he knew very well: the sexy walk of his secretary, Trish.

'Oh bum,' Tom remarked, 'he's only meeting Trish. Whatever is she doing here?'

'Perhaps she's trying to sell him some paintings?'

Tom turned on his friend. 'What on earth do you mean, Trevor?'

Trevor smiled. 'How do you think someone could walk into a police station with documents signed by you unless they had access to your letter heading and experience of signing your name on them?'

Tom shook his head with disbelief; no, not Trish – his partner of over five years, who had shared his bed and everything else.

Trevor placed his hand gently on Tom's arm. 'Let's watch and see what develops.'

As Tom and Trevor observed them, the attitude of Jonathan suddenly changed to one of rage; he was shouting at Trish as if in reaction to some unnerving news! What on earth could she be telling him? Tom and Trevor continued their observation of Tom's partners in both senses – his lady of five years and his present art partner who looked from that distance as if he was rather upset. As the two men watched, Jonathan's demeanour suddenly changed and he grabbed Trish with a bear hug, kissing her on the mouth as if she had suddenly given him a million pounds – perhaps she had! Then they got up from the table and walked to the car park, stopping at Trish's rented car to look at something in the boot. Jonathan seemed satisfied and reached in his pocket.

'I imagine you might just get a phone call from Jonathan cancelling your appointment this afternoon,' Trevor remarked. As if on cue, Tom's phone rang and, sure enough, it was Jonathan suggesting that they cancel the appointment for a few days in order that he could make some enquiries if anyone was offering the paintings around.

'Yes, that sounds a good idea, Jonathan.' Tom replaced his phone in his pocket. 'You're not bad at this yourself, Trevor – you must be psychic!'

Trevor grinned. 'Yes, it must be catching, this cops and robbers game we're playing.' Tom looked at Trevor – God, he just doesn't realise what is involved – the millions of euros that are at stake!

Chapter Twenty-Two

Jonathan and Trish arrived back at the hotel and, after using the hotel room for a few hours making up for some of the lost time and leaving them both extremely satisfied with their efforts, Jonathan called Louis to arrange another appointment with the Cardinal. Louis was pleased to hear that they could press ahead with the appointment. He had been around long enough to know that there must have been some problem but, in his relaxed, quiet way, he would bide his time until everything came back on line. Art makes you that way; not only does the beauty of some pictures relax you, there is also an art to waiting for the next masterpiece to show up.

Trish and Jonathan sat in an out-of-the-way restaurant talking earnestly about how Trish had suddenly decided to pull off the master stroke of obtaining the paintings for them. She had already explained that, after hearing what Tom had got up to trying to cheat Jonathan out of his fair share of commission, she had been upset and wanted to even things up by taking the pictures. After all, it was going to be their nest egg!

Jonathan was pleased to hear this; it gave him great assurance that here, for once in his life, he had a lady who wanted to be with him. He knew that, if she ever found out he had been responsible for the 'kidnapping' of her; she would not be too pleased. Well, to be fair she had never ever been kidnapped really; just delayed in the cabin so he could give certain people the impression that she had been taken. Either way, Jonathan would make every effort to ensure that no one ever knew about any of that!

He received confirmation of the appointment at the Vatican which surprisingly was the next day. He called up the airport and booked two seats on the evening flight to the USA. He knew they could not hang around and face bumping into Tom Rendell.

The three arrived at the Vatican and were ushered into the presence of the Cardinal where, as usual, the paintings were examined very closely. Jonathan made a plausible excuse that Tom had been taken ill and was letting him act for both of them.

The excitement generated by the three experts was evident and, when the usual nods were exchanged, the Cardinal announced that the sum of twenty-two million euros would be the price set for the purchase of the three paintings – was that satisfactory?

Jonathan beamed at Trish, Louis and then at the Cardinal. 'Yes, Your Eminence, that will be quite satisfactory!'

His Eminence got up and left them. Jonathan and Trish smiled broadly. They could not believe their good fortune. Louis said he was going take his leave; the Clerk would be coming in to arrange the transfer of funds. Jonathan nodded; he realised that he would have to change the normal bank details which he had to hand. The Clerk to the Vatican came in, sat down and wrote out a cheque for twenty-two million euros! Jonathan grabbed it and counted the numbers, then the figures… they looked great… but… 'Sir, you've made the cheque out to Madame Connie Pasteur… that is incorrect!'

The man looked straight at Jonathan and Trish. 'No, sir, it is correct according to this man here.' He pointed to the door.

Jonathan turned to the door and gasped as Tom and Trevor

emerged with smiles on their faces. 'Hullo, Jonathan. Oh, and you, Trish. It was really nice of you to recover the paintings for us. We understand the rightful owner, Connie Pasteur, is very anxious to reward you both for your efforts. I believe you will find the enclosed acceptable – two first-class airline tickets made out in your names for the evening flight to the United States of America – that is, of course, unless you would prefer to spend some time in an Italian jail?'

Jonathan looked daggers at Tom. Trish went as white as a sheet; she could not look Tom in the face as he approached her and, lifting her face in his hand, said, 'Trish, I would not have seen you wanting – you know that!'

Trish and Jonathan left with the two policemen who would accompany them to the airport and put them on the flight to the USA. Tom thanked the Clerk and, placing the cheque in his pocket, left the building with his friend – amateur detective Trevor Miles.

Outside, he glanced at Trevor. 'I reckon we managed that quite well, Trevor. What say we collect Cassie and make a night of it. Oh, by the way, I reckon the Countess will be happy to award you a sizeable reward for your part in recovering the pictures – it's the least she can do.'

Trevor was about to respond when Ben suddenly strolled up to them and, looking straight at Trevor, exclaimed, 'That turned out well, sir, didn't it.'

'Yes it did, Ben. Please thank the men for all their efforts and, by the way, ask them all to be at the hotel at eight o'clock – the evening's on this gentleman.' He pointed at a bemused Tom.

'Why did he call you sir? What did he mean, Trevor? What men? Who is treating who?' Tom continued with his questions.

Trevor took Tom by his arm and guided him back to the

car. 'Well, it's like this, Tom, I have to admit that, when you arranged the mortgage for the house you sold us, I was a little bit lenient with the truth… you see…'

The rest of the conversation was lost as Rome's evening rush-hour traffic intensified. The relationship between the two friends would never be quite the same!

Cassie looked radiant that evening with her specially purchased evening dress which fitted in all the correct places but at the same time also showing off the class of the lady wearing it. The three of them sat at the table waiting on Trevor's colleagues to join them. The news about Trish and Jonathan had been greeted by Cassie with some amazement. However, this paled when Tom, with an embarrassed look at Trevor, suddenly took out of his pocket a ring box which he placed in front of Cassie.

'Cassie, I guess I had better make an honest woman of you – if you don't mind – I mean, if you will have me?'

The amazement on her face turned into a beaming smile. 'Yes, Tom, of course I will, and by the way I have something to tell you!'

She bent over and whispered in Tom's ear.

'You can't be serious, Cassie. Are you sure?'

On the other side of the table, Trevor laughed as he looked at their surprised faces. 'Well, Tom, all I can say is perhaps you had better stay selling houses, because you're no good at knowing you are about to become a father!'

'How the heck did you know?'

'Well, my old mate, I don't work for MI5 for nothing! Besides, having three children, I do know when a lady has that certain glow on her face which can only mean one thing; you'll have to sell even more houses now!'

Chapter Twenty-Three

Life at the château of Madame Pasteur had been rather difficult since Connie had received the extremely polite letter from a Madame Cassie Rendell informing her that her husband, Mr Tom Rendell, would not be able to represent her in regard to selling any further paintings, now or in the future.

One morning, not long after Cassie's letter had been received, Madame Connie's household staff sat glumly at the table in the spacious kitchen, chatting over an early morning cup of tea.

'What's she like today, Anna?'

'The same, Daniel.'

'Any chance of him coming back?'

'Doesn't look like it.'

'Then I think I'm going to look for a new position!'

Daniel and Anna were long-established servants to the Pasteur household having joined its service just before the death of Monsieur Pasteur six years before. They had grown used to the volatile behaviour of their mistress, Connie Pasteur who, when things were going her way, always treated all her staff well. However, when things did not, it was quite a different story.

All had seemed well earlier that morning when she had surprised the staff in the kitchen by asking for two boiled eggs and toast. The normal procedure would have been a much more relaxed breakfast, with Madame Pasteur arriving in the breakfast room around 8.30 a.m. and perusing the printed menu of the day.

Connie's arrival that morning did not comply with her usual carefully maintained immaculate appearance. Her hair was in total disarray and her make-up had obviously been left on from the night before. As far as her clothing was concerned, all that was missing was evidence of the previous morning's breakfast. Her robe was crumpled and grubby and despite Stella, her chambermaid, laying out newly laundered clothes for her, the mistress had chosen to wear the same apparel she had worn all that week. Was the lady in mourning or something? Anna wondered.

Daniel pressed for more information. 'So what exactly happened in the kitchen this morning?'

Anna looked perplexed, 'No one is sure, but as the staff placed her breakfast tray on the kitchen table, she seemed to go berserk! It did seem that just looking at the table reminded her of something or someone... and she just lost it!'

Daniel, puzzled, raised his eyebrows as if to say – but why?

Anna giggled. 'You've heard about the early morning table bonk with a certain person who will remain anonymous, but his initials are TR, haven't you?'

It was Daniel's turn to laugh. 'Oh, that one!'

Their cosy chat was interrupted by the harsh tones of their mistress who suddenly appeared at the top of the grand staircase and shouted down to the kitchen. 'Tell Arthur Thomas to come and see me. Now.'

Anna jumped to her feet. 'Yes, Madame; straightaway,' she called.

'Good grief,' Daniel gasped. 'Arthur Thomas is still out – he went out with Susan from the village shop.'

'So you'd best give him a call on his mobile, hadn't you,' Anna replied, 'and tell him to get his backside up here pronto!'

*

Arthur Thomas, hearing the ring of his mobile phone, reached across and answered. He had just spent the night, courtesy of his girlfriend Susan's father, in the room above the garage near the village shop. Thanking Daniel for the information, he quickly finished dressing and went down the rickety stairs which led to the side entrance of the garage. He was met there by Susan who was in the process of bringing him a cup of coffee and a croissant.

Taking the croissant from Susan's hand and eating it as he walked to his car, he said, 'Sorry, Susan, I have to leave straightaway and get back to the château – it seems I'm wanted by the boss!'

Susan's face showed her disappointment; she had been hoping to spend a few hours with the handsome young Englishman who had only recently plucked up the courage to ask her out. Susan worked at the village shop owned by her father and mother. The family also owned a small farm that supplied all the fresh produce to the shop on a daily basis. Despite being one of the prettiest girls in the small village, Susan had remained single and, as far as her father was concerned, while that state of affairs continued she would remain a virgin, for if she was to marry one of the rich landowners in the vicinity, she was going to have to be pure. Her strict father would make sure of it!

Susan, for her part, had gone along with it all these years because, for one thing, she had not had the opportunity to do otherwise and, for another, until now she had not found anyone she wanted to do it with! At twenty-five years of age, Susan still gave the impression of being an extremely innocent young lady and, to ensure she stayed that way, her father had last night given the small bed over the garage to her would-be lover and locked up his daughter in the main house.

Arthur Thomas Stevens had arrived in the area five years ago and spent a year working at the château as a chauffeur for the Pasteurs. To the Countess, who normally only addressed her staff by their last names, Arthur Thomas was often shortened to his initials, so AT he had become. He had left to attend an art course at a Paris university, and at the age of twenty-eight, he had recently returned to work at the château, again as the chauffeur.

Kissing Susan on the cheek, he made his farewell with a promise to call later that day when time permitted. Susan waved goodbye – half wishing that she had taken the risk of visiting the room above the garage as she had been invited to do by the handsome Englishman – but one thing that Susan did fear more than any other was the wrath of her puritanical father.

Arthur arrived at the château with a smile on his face and seeing Daniel's enquiring look as to how the evening had gone, he smirked and tried to give the impression that he had managed to score a home run! Daniel, who had a lot of experience of village life, knew instinctively that the young Englishman was telling a bit of a porky, as the English say!

Arthur had not taken more than ten steps into the grand hall when his mistress, the Countess, called out his name: 'AT, get up here – now!' Arthur entered the bedroom and surveyed the scattered bedclothes of Madame Connie – the lady had spent a restless night!

Connie approached her chauffeur and looked him straight in the eye. 'Did you have a nice evening off, Arthur?'

Arthur nodded.

'Did you meet anyone nice, Arthur dear?'

Arthur immediately knew where all this was leading.

He had experienced it once before when he first arrived at the château. He knew that there was only one correct answer for his jealous mistress. 'No, just a boring evening at the local village bar – all on my own, Madame Connie.'

'Oh, what a shame.' The Countess smiled. 'Well, we must do something about that mustn't we.' Nodding to Arthur's clothes, she said, 'Better to take it all off!'

Arthur knew that when Madame Connie wanted something she normally got what she wanted and, this morning, what Madame Connie wanted was him!

Downstairs, Daniel turned to Anna. 'I guess you'd better inform the kitchen staff that breakfast will be late this morning, but to also pray that our Arthur Thomas does us all a big favour and puts a smile back on our mistress's face or we'll be in for another day of upset.'

Chapter Twenty-Four

Trevor Miles was with Paul Jansen in one of the local restaurants in the London suburb of Islington. He had related to Paul how well the wedding of his friend Tom Rendell had gone and how lovely his bride Cassie had looked. The inevitable question of the paintings came up and Trevor was able to give his boss a full account of how the pictures had been stolen and then recovered. The hard part came when Paul brought up the question of who owned what. Why had the Vatican, after buying the first two, refused the next three, only to then go ahead with the purchase of them? Tom had told Trevor that Connie had confided in him that the paintings were the real thing having been obtained, stolen if you will, during the last war. It seemed that, long before the war started, several extremely talented people had copied the originals and then sold the copies to certain museums and organisations. A few private collectors had also been conned into thinking that they actually owned an original. Tom had indicated that the Mona Lisa in Paris could also be a good copy!

Paul looked at Trevor in amazement. 'Are you sure about this, Trevor?'

'That's what Tom said. I have no reason to disbelieve him though I suppose it is conceivable that Madame Pasteur might be telling lies.'

'I think we had better visit Tom's Madame Connie as soon as possible, because if this gets out our Government could be embarrassed if anyone found out that we had any inkling of this and did nothing about it! Better tell Allison that you have to go to Europe again on stockbroker business. It's unfortunate that your friend Rendell knows you're MI5, but I suppose it can't be helped.'

Trevor nodded, feeling safe in the knowledge that Tom had kept his real job a secret.

Jessica had returned to Paris after giving her blessing to the marriage of Tom and Cassie. Cassie, wishing to make friends with her again, had invited her to be her matron of honour and Jessica had been only too willing to oblige. While at the wedding, she had taken time to give some advice to Cassie about a certain Countess in France whom Jessica thought should be given her marching orders, just in case a certain amorous boss chose to take up where he had left off. As far as Jessica was concerned, if she could not have Tom again, she would make darn sure that the rich bitch would not have him either. Cassie was only too eager to do as her friend advised; hence the letter to Madame Connie. Tom felt a little disappointed hearing this. He had enjoyed the angry sex that had taken place a few months ago on a certain kitchen table. However, with the impending birth of his son, as a scan had revealed, he knew he had to behave – well for the time being at least! There also was the problem that he was very much in love with his new wife Cassie; how the mighty had fallen!

Connie was rather surprised to hear from Trevor about the impending visit by himself and his boss. Trevor had not gone into any detail, but Connie realised that her secret about the paintings was out. Naturally, the payment of millions of euros had been extremely welcome, but she did regret the loss of

Tom Rendell's excellent services. However, she had to admit that AT, her substitute lover, had performed extremely well under the circumstances and at such short notice too! Yes, Madame Connie had a smile on her face again, much to the relief of the staff at the château.

Tom and Cassie returned from their honeymoon in Spain having decided to have two residences, one in Windsor and the other in Italy. Tom realized for the first time that his life would never be the same; having a wife and soon to become a father. Tom Rendell the stud was now a responsible family man for the first time in his life.

Trevor and Paul arrived at the château around noon to find that Connie had made an extra effort for their visit. Lunch had been prepared on the large veranda that surrounded the château and soon the two men were totally engrossed with their hostess. Trevor could readily see how Tom had succumbed to her charms. Paul, for his part, was equally captivated by her and was leaning forward listening to her every word. No one mentioned Tom Rendell and it was late afternoon before Paul and Trevor decided they should at least explain the reason for their visit.

Connie was by now pulling out all the stops; firstly turning her attentions on Paul and then Trevor, as if to discover whose Achilles' heel was exposed. First she thought it would be Paul, but then perhaps Trevor. Either way she realised that she must choose or she would not be in a position to split the two men. Connie knew that an adversary split would be a problem halved. With grace, she went through the motions of being the misunderstood lady; for the first time she mentioned Tom, the sharp-talking art expert who had managed to persuade her to sell her paintings, paintings which had been in her family for more years than she could remember. By God, he had been extremely persuasive, convincing this lonely widow, who had nobody in the world to turn to, that he alone was the one to help her to get out of poverty and become solvent again.

Hallelujah! Thank God for Tom Rendell, Trevor thought. This was certainly a side of him that Trevor did not know about – in fact it was fortunate that he had known his friend for so many years or he would certainly have been tempted to ask this Rendell fellow to save him as well! God, she was good, this lady was good! Trevor looked at Paul to see his reaction to this load of tripe, but Paul just smiled and nodded as if he approved and understood everything the Frenchwoman was saying.

The final nail in the coffin was when the Countess denied even having a secret room. The five pictures sold by Tom for her were originally hung on the staircase walls, she said. She walked to the staircase and indicated each empty space where they had hung.

The way Madame Connie's hips managed to sway as she walked, coupled with her delicate perfumed scent, which always hung seductively in the air everywhere she went, was not lost on the two men.

Poor Tom Rendell, he must have misheard her, she asserted. Secret room indeed; how on earth had he arrived at that conclusion?

The two men, realising that she was not going to admit anything that evening, made their goodbyes and left. Trevor, leading the way, did not see the note which Madame Connie managed to slip into the hand offered by Paul. She had made her choice and it certainly did not include Trevor!

Chapter Twenty-Five

Feeling much weaker than when he had entered it, Arthur Thomas left the bedroom shaking his head and marvelling at his lady boss's stamina. Good grief, she had just increased his sex education tenfold! Where had she learnt all those positions? The woman was an animal! He suddenly felt like a grand headhunter; yes, and another notch on his bedpost. He failed to see that the trophy case in the Countess's bedroom now held another scalp!

Later, he looked in the mirror at the deep scratches on his back and realised that he had to hide the spoils of war from his new girlfriend Susan; that is, if he got so lucky!

Trevor was surprised to learn that his boss had received a text message asking him to stop off at the office in Paris. He naturally thought they would be returning in his car via the Tunnel that evening. After all, Paul knew that Trevor had a birthday party to go to, his daughter's tenth.

'Don't worry, Trevor, you go ahead and attend your daughter's party – I'll catch the first flight back in the morning,' Paul said.

Trevor did as he was instructed and managed to catch the next car freight out which would enable him to be home in plenty of time for his daughter's birthday. Sometimes it does work out well for the hard-pressed guardians of the peace, he thought to himself as he sped home.

Still in France, Paul Jansen arrived back at the château by taxi and, paying the driver, knocked politely on the large doors of the house. This was greeted by a scene which, in the light of the numerous spluttering candles, gave out one signal – and that, he decided, was green for go!

Jessica continued her work in the Paris office hoping that, one day, her Prince Charming would turn up. After all, she had in the past made do with the infrequent visits of her boss. Now he appeared to be permanently occupied, she hoped that one day a new man would show up on the scene. Trish, as daft as she had been, had managed to land a new man in the form of art dealer Jonathan; if nothing else, he must have satisfied her in the right places.

Late one evening, when she was about to shut the office, a good-looking man walked in and introduced himself as Giorgio. He was most apologetic and, seeing that Jessica was about to close, quickly indicated he wanted to purchase a property in Paris. He would, however, wait until the next day to talk with her further. In the meantime, could he take her to dinner, that is, if there was no Mr Jessica? He added this after reading her name tag displayed on her ample bosom.

Jessica's eyes gleamed and, upon shutting the office door, she offered up her silent thanks to the heavens: 'Thank you, God!' Treating the stranger to her warmest smile, she readily accepted his invitation and catching hold of his arm led him to her favourite Italian restaurant. Since he was a prospective client, she explained, she would be the one doing the taking. Her expense account was more than adequate for dealing with new clients – especially handsome Italians, she added under her breath. She was enjoying herself and it was with hidden pleasure that she chose the most outrageously expensive

French wines in honour of her guest. Aside from the fact that she wasn't that keen on the Italian stuff, there were many ways to reap revenge and, if you couldn't do it one way, then hit them where you can – in their pockets. Tom Rendell owed her that much at least.

Paul Jansen thought he was in a different world. He was the one who rarely went out into the field; he left that to Trevor and the others. His job was to collate all the data that streamed onto his desk at MI5. As he was single, he had always devoted much of his time to his work. The so-called dalliance with Russian and German female spies, as illustrated in all the 007 films, did not happen in real life; at least, not in the closeted world of Paul Jansen who was, he supposed, the equivalent of 'M' in the Bond films.

Madame Connie, having weighed up the situation and made her choice, now knew everything she needed to know about her new guest. There was no seductive warm fire and white rug in the lounge – just one suggestion: that Paul joined her upstairs in her private room where she would show him other works of art that up to now she had never shown a living soul. It underlined the fact that poor Tom Rendell was not only dead in the water; he was by now apparently laid out cold.

Paul followed his hostess up to her bedroom and looked around as if to confront the array of works that no living soul had ever seen – he could not see any artwork at all. He had no time to dwell on this latest revelation before he found himself being led to the en suite bathroom with its subdued lighting. Madame Connie removed his jacket and pulled expertly at his tie. It was blatantly obvious that she'd had prior experience of doing this. Paul gulped as next to follow were his socks. What the heck was the woman doing – what about the rest of his clothes? As if to spare his blushes, Connie led him into the large 'his and her' shower cubicle and turned on the taps, just enough to dampen his clothes but not his ardour. In a magical moment, Paul found that his hostess had somehow managed to lose her gown, letting it slip to the floor just before entering the cubicle. Now he was the only one with any clothing on, but not for long. Slowly but surely, Connie expertly disrobed her guest one garment at a time – but stopping short of removing his close-fitting jockey shorts. For now, they were going to stay; apparently it was taboo to go any further. Momentarily embarrassed by his very obvious, rock-hard erection and not sure what might happen next, Paul felt like a fly caught in a web. The black widow spider had secured her victim, closed the door and was preparing to devour her prey. Paul, or Mr M as he was known to his colleagues, was about to experience the real world. Take it or leave it – there was no way out.

Chapter Twenty-Six

Jessica looked intently at Giorgio and could see that he was much older than she; in fact he could well be older than her boss. His dark eyes seemed to encase her as they swept over her and twinkled in admiration. Jessica blushed as this stranger continued his intense and relentless scrutiny of her. She could not remember anyone, not even Tom Rendell, paying her such attention. Giorgio also knew how to treat a lady. His words and actions were all designed to please and excite; the light stroking of her arms as he pulled her chair to the table, the touch on her shoulders as he asked if she was warm enough.

Warm! Jessica was getting hotter by the minute and they had not even started on their home-made hot tomato soup!

If this keeps up, she thought, she would not sell this man a house – she would give the bastard one! What was he doing – didn't he realise that she was on the rebound and as horny as hell?

The clinking of glasses was surely just the sound of things to come; any thoughts of Tom Rendell, master sex-machine-cum-man-about-town, were finishing up in one place: the waste bin. It would seem that her boss's influence was declining by the minute each time Giorgio spoke, compliments falling from his lips as his dark brown eyes caressed her. How did the saying go – another one bites the dust? The King is dead – long live the King. Or to put it another way: Tom Rendell – you're history!

*

In Connie's en suite, Paul Jansen's legs were all of a quiver. He was sure that they would not support his body as his host turned her attention to his wet, closely fitting jockey shorts. She started to remove them just as you would peel an orange – one section at a time, pulling them further down, stopping as if to view the scene, continuing only when she could see the effect that her actions were having. Paul's lack of field experience was being tested to the limit – what if he failed? This prospect did not bear thinking about and he gritted his teeth as he felt her soft hand firmly grasping and cupping his balls and stroking his penis. It was torture of the most exquisite kind. Good grief, if the woman didn't stop doing what she was doing, she might just find that he would give her more than she bargained for – and that hadn't happened to him since he was a teenager. The prospect of a sudden fierce spray came constantly closer with her every move. Spray? Paul thought wryly – it could well be an eruption.

He need not have worried. The lady may be a tramp but she was certainly an experienced tramp. She did not want Paul to conclude his part of the proceedings too soon and she knew exactly when to stop. Tucking everything neatly back into its original place in his sodden jockey shorts, she slithered back up his body kissing every part at will.

'Everything comes to he who waits,' Connie teased, apparently wanting to make sure her 'guest' remained in heaven just that little bit longer.

Jessica was bearing up better but only just – Giorgio had just finished feeding her the dessert of strawberries; broken gently into two by his strong white teeth and passed seductively over the dining table. How naff was that? It might look good in the pictures, but in real life – surely not! Jessica didn't care; she was enjoying everything and she had not had so much attention since God knows when. No, if Giorgio kept this up, he might well achieve something that she had rarely done before on the first date – allow him to come home with her to show her what he could do in more comfortable surroundings. Who was she trying to kid? If all else failed, she'd kidnap him!

Trevor had tried to contact his boss several times but had finally given up. He had several ideas that he wanted to discuss and he knew Paul would wish to hear them while they were still fresh in his mind. His boss was a stickler for timing. If you had anything on your mind, Paul was the first person who wanted to hear it. He always said that first impressions count. Trevor turned his attention back to his family and, after putting his children to bed early, he whispered in Allison's ear that perhaps they should also have an early night. Allison was pleasantly surprised when her husband, who normally did his three minutes and then rolled over, went on and on; he was magnificent.

For his part, Trevor, a happily married man, try as he might, could not get the recurring vision of a certain lady's swaying posterior out of his mind. Feeling just a little guilty, he was aware that it added a certain spice to his marital performance.

Had Trevor managed to reach his boss, he might not have received the response he expected. In fact it was more likely to have been 'Not now you idiot' because, while Trevor was envisaging Connie's seductive swaying, his boss was experiencing it at first-hand. Paul was a happy bunny; the kissing had stopped – on the lips at least. He was now receiving close attention of another kind. He gasped as Connie's warm lips continued to tease his erection, holding him on a knife-edge of exquisite agony. He had long ago lost his wet jockey shorts and it was now open season for anything or anyone who might choose to close in on any part of his trembling body. His eyes swivelled in their sockets as the pressure intensified and he found himself gazing at the soft lighting above him. Paul had surprised himself; one of the stalwarts of Her Majesty's Government, he was going to a place where he had never gone before. He was on an incredible journey; one which he craved would never stop. Had he known about Arthur Thomas's conclusion that Connie Pasteur was indeed an animal, he might well have readily agreed but, at that moment, his thoughts remained in dreamland.

With one easy action, Connie swirled her prey out of the double shower cubicle and straight onto the spacious bathroom floor. Paul gasped as he found himself spreadeagled on the tiles with what could only be described as a screaming banshee on top of him, groaning loudly as she rode out her immediate desires. If Connie was missing her estate agent lover, she did not show it. She was indulging in something that had served her well in the past – angry sex.

As Paul finally came to, in every sense of the word, all he could do was to remain where he had fallen, convinced he had died and gone to heaven. In a daze, he watched as Connie, with a disdainful glance in his direction, stood up and walked away from him, as if to say, 'Take that, you bastard!' There was no doubt in Paul's mind that the lady was a tramp – but an extremely sexy one at that.

It was Monday morning and time for most people to recognise that they have to work. Work was something that Tom Rendell had quietly forgotten about. He knew that he had accumulated another three million euros, having been able to retain the commission that would have gone to Jonathan. Tom had contacted Louis who, knowing fully what had happened, just told him to keep all the commission for himself. That disturbed Tom a bit and, despite the American's complicity in stealing the paintings, he felt a little guilty. After all, Jonathan had introduced Louis to him in the first place and set up the sale to the Vatican. On the other hand, the man was a crook. Apparently there would be no more paintings to sell – unless, of course, he could persuade Madame Pasteur to sell some more. When he ventured to mention this possibility to Cassie, she just coughed and Tom realised that, were he ever to consider such a move, it could well be considered suicidal on his part – at least as far as his marriage was concerned.

Jessica opened her eyes and wondered where she was. Then she realised that she was not in her own bed; of that she was sure. She could recall leaving the restaurant with Giorgio and being kissed just before getting into a car. She frowned; she could not remember a thing about it. She must have drunk far too much of that expensive wine. She looked around and took note of the surroundings. Goodness, she was in a rather tatty hotel bedroom by the look of it. Her companion of the evening before was absent. Where had he gone? She could see the bathroom was empty; no sign of anyone taking a shower. Getting out of bed, she realised that all she had on was her bra – nothing else. Whatever had happened last night, it must have involved sex – but with whom? Was it Giorgio – she certainly hoped it was not anyone else. At least she did remember fancying him. Standing up did nothing to help sort out her throbbing head and her legs didn't seem to want to hold her up. Some hangover; she had never felt quite this bad before. She sat down again quickly on the side of the bed. She was about to make another attempt to get to the bathroom when the bedroom door opened and a smiling Giorgio entered.

'Oh, I see you are finally awake my little sex machine – you certainly know how to entertain your clients!'

Blushing, Jessica inwardly cursed that if indeed she had done what this man was indicating, she would like to have at least some memory of it. What a waste!

'Come,' he said with laugh, 'let us get some breakfast and then you can show me Paris and some of those lovely properties you were telling me about last night.'

Good grief, Jessica thought. She could not remember telling him about anything – properties or anything else. What must he think of her? Embarrassed, she scuttled into the shower and, after several minutes under the hot, gushing water, she finally began to feel a little better. Her head was clearing and she was certainly much more surefooted than when she had first got out of bed. As she turned off the shower, she heard someone speaking. Opening the bathroom door, she just caught the closing words of Giorgio. He had been talking into his mobile and appeared to be explaining to somebody that it had all gone very well and he would be in touch.

Seeing Jessica's enquiring gaze, Giorgio quickly explained that he had just finished talking to his office in Rome. He went on to tell her that he was the deputy manager of a company called 'Electroco' which dealt in electronic equipment He was being relocated to Paris to open up a new office and the first step would be for him to purchase an apartment or house. Either way, Giorgio thought that the welcome that she had afforded him had been excellent in every way.

Jessica accompanied him to the breakfast room, still trying to remember anything that would make some sense of the night of passion that he seemed to remember so well, but as far as she was concerned – nothing!

Chapter Twenty-Seven

Paul Jansen was also now recovering from his night of passion with the Countess, but unlike Jessica he could remember just about everything. He had no reason to know about the usual procedure that was followed when men were entertained at the château; the personal valet service that took place before they had even managed to come to from their night's efforts. In Paul's case, his suit that had received such rough treatment had been cleaned and neatly pressed; his shirt and even his tie was immaculate and what was it that he could feel in his trouser pocket? Taking the box out, he was pleasantly surprised to see it contained some incredibly smart diamond cufflinks.

He put them on immediately; he would be gracious in accepting them. After all, he thought he had performed quite well and if the lady of the house wished to give him a small gift then the least he could do was to show his appreciation.

History repeated itself that morning. He was welcomed like any other businessman who had stayed overnight on business, invited to choose from the daily printed menu which was conveniently positioned by his place at the long breakfast table.

Connie addressed him rather tersely. 'Well, Mr Jansen, what was it you wanted to see me about?'

Taken aback, Paul looked at his hostess. It seemed she had completely forgotten all that had happened the night before or that he was there at her invitation. It was as if, as far as

Madame Pasteur was concerned, what was past had passed. This was a new day and it was business as usual – thank you and goodbye. Dumbfounded, Paul hastily swallowed his breakfast, made the appropriate noises of gratitude and took his leave in the waiting taxi.

Connie smiled as she waved last night's conquest goodbye – yes, that should take care of it. How easy it was for these government bodies to be compromised. She was sure last night's sexual exploits were now firmly imprinted on the man's brain. It wouldn't take much to refresh his memory and, failing that, a copy of the video that had recorded everything that had taken place that night, in both bathroom and bedroom, would suffice. It was a shame, she reflected, that she had not turned it on when Tom had been there – she would have liked to have been able to review that evening again when she was feeling particularly horny. Connie had reasoned that, in Tom's particular case, it would have been too risky having such a tape – in the event that one day she might have to deny even knowing him. Video recordings are alright – but only when they serve the right purpose.

As she went about her business that day, she did wonder briefly if she would need to invite that Trevor person to the château. He was obviously very much married and the one thing Madame Connie did love was a challenge.

Paul caught the next flight back to London. The only thing he had accomplished was to get laid. That, he had to admit, had been out of this world and quite beyond his experience, but as far as finding out anything else went, other than discovering that the Frenchwoman was a nymphomaniac, he had utterly failed. He hoped Trevor would not ask too many questions, but glancing at his missed calls list on his mobile he feared the worst. His lapse would not be easy to explain; Paul Jansen had spelt it out time and time again that his staff must be contactable every minute of the day and night. For the first time in his long and distinguished career, Mr M had broken his own golden rule – several times over – and he felt decidedly guilty.

Jessica dropped off her client, Giorgio, at his hotel. He had seen many properties that day but seemed unable to make up his mind which one he preferred. He would have to meet up with her again tomorrow. Jessica was a little disappointed that he never made any attempt to ask her up to his hotel room. That might have enabled her to remember something of the night before. Had she been good; had she managed to satisfy him; had he satisfied her? Good grief, what had she been drinking that night to pass out in that way? Whatever it was, it had certainly left her with a huge headache.

The next day, she was pleasantly surprised to receive a phone call from him stating he had come to a conclusion about one of the properties and if she would start the paperwork he could complete the purchase within the next five days. Jessica was pleased; it had been a lean few months and she had not managed to sell anything. This was her first sale for some time. At least the commission would help pay her monthly rent. It also gave her the excuse to contact Tom and tell him the good news. In normal circumstances it would have meant him coming to Paris to oversee the final paperwork. That would be nice – perhaps she might be able to… her imagination started running riot as she recalled some of her past sexual encounters with her boss. Her face flushed and she shook her head; just the thought made her hormones go into overdrive – and just when she'd thought she'd put him in the waste bin; damn the man.

Tom sounded pleased to hear Jessica's good news. He said he would be coming to Paris the following week and asked her to book a double room in the usual hotel. Jessica readily agreed, her heart missing a beat as she thought of their encounter when he last visited. Ooh la la! She did find it strange to have such thoughts when she should have been quite satisfied after last night – had Giorgio done his bit? There again, Tom always did have a big effect on her when she was in his presence.

Paul and Trevor sat in the café outside their office discussing the visit to Madame Connie; Paul, of course, leaving out the very latest episode that had occurred. After all, it would not add much to the overall state of things. He was also not sure that his colleague would understand that he had mixed business with such immense pleasure.

Trevor was confirming that they had not achieved anything. Madame Connie had kept her secret about the paintings extremely well and the only person who might make her admit to anything was probably Tom Rendell. How they could get him involved again was not clear. Trevor knew about Cassie's feeling on the matter – it was, as far as she was concerned, a no-go. Paul, however, was not in the mood for taking no action at all – he had to redeem himself. He asked Trevor to contact Tom and organise a meeting with the two of them in Paris. Arrangements could then be made for them to confront the Countess. Trevor agreed, deciding he would call Tom on his mobile rather than pay a visit to the family home. He certainly did not wish to be present when Tom broke the news to Cassie.

Tom's response was fine. He was in fact going to Paris that very weekend to meet Jessica in order to finalise a sale she had just made. They could all meet up before or even after the sale had been completed. Paul, pleased to hear this, asked Trevor to contact Madame Pasteur to arrange a further meeting.

Jessica was sitting at her desk when the call came in from her boss; not only would she be seeing Tom, but also Trevor and his superior, Paul. She would have to arrange two more rooms at the hotel. Damn, she thought – that would likely put an end to any romantic notions she was harbouring.

Connie was not happy to receive the request for yet another meeting – she thought she had precluded any further action. Her staff soon found that their volatile mistress was not in a good temper and, what was more, there was no Arthur Thomas to help change her mood – he was too busy pursuing Susan, the farmer's daughter.

Paul arrived early at the office; he wanted to clear some of his in tray before he went to Paris to meet up with Trevor and Tom, then on to a further meeting with Madame Connie. He wondered if she would acknowledge that anything had taken place between them but, given her behaviour the morning after the night before, he thought it unlikely.

Checking his post, which had already been sorted by his secretary, he came to a small package addressed to him personally. Julie, his secretary, said it had gone through the usual X-ray security checks and it seemed that it was indeed a DVD, not a bomb, which was reassuring! He did not recognise the handwriting and idly put the disc into his computer and pressed the run button. Large close-ups followed – scenes that he instantly recognised: his loss of apparel – his loss of everything including his dignity.

The oldest trick in the book and he, 'M' of the British

Secret Service, had fallen for it – hook, line and sinker. The sink part was his stomach, which turned over and over again. The meaning was clear – leave well enough alone. The bitch!

Paul picked up his phone and autodialled Trevor – he had to stop this investigation going any further. His mind was in turmoil as he sought desperately to come up with a plausible excuse to pull his man off the case. He didn't feel too guilty. After all, he reasoned, this was not an issue of national security; just a mix-up in the art world that should, more properly, be investigated by Interpol. There was no reason why he shouldn't keep his head down on this one.

In Paris, Trevor had met Tom and Jessica at the café just around the corner from the office. Jessica should not have worried about losing out with Trevor being there – Tom already had a chaperon: Cassie! She was looking very pregnant and, as with most pregnant women, glowing with a certain radiance. Jessica cursed silently to herself; she realised that her boss must be turning cartwheels not having his usual weekly sexual exercise – she would have loved to put a big smile on his face.

Within minutes, along came the ever-smiling Giorgio, briefcase in his hand and an obvious desire to get on quickly with the transaction. Introducing Tom and Trevor to him, Jessica was pleased to have at least something to take her mind off her disappointment – at least her bank balance would improve, even if her bodily needs would not. She was also a little gratified to see what she was sure was a fleeting glance of jealousy flit across Tom's face.

After a brief inspection of the house in question, they retired to one of the restaurants in town for the signing and paying of the deposit. This system, as used throughout Europe, meant that Giorgio had twenty-eight days to pay the balance and it would then be totally his. As the wine flowed, the party, including Trevor, all started to enjoy themselves. Trevor, having put his mobile on mute, did not hear Paul's vain attempt to contact him. It was nice to relax again with his friend Tom in Paris, with Jessica and the new buyer Giorgio who just happened to be one of the nicest people one could meet.

Some while later, realising that Cassie was getting tired, Tom made their excuses and they went to their hotel room. As Cassie was expecting the baby in three weeks, it had been decided that Jessica would stay with her while Tom accompanied Trevor and Paul – assuming that Paul showed up – for the showdown with Madame Connie.

It was left to Jessica to explain to Giorgio that they must curtail their pleasant meeting as Tom and his colleagues had to get to an important business meeting the next day, and Cassie needed her company while they were gone. Giorgio had no problem with that. Thanking her for the excellent dinner, he left the restaurant and went on his way. Watching him go, Jessica smiled to herself. At least something good had come out of the day – yes, sometimes things did go right for struggling salespeople.

Chapter Twenty-Eight

The Countess was fuming. She had just received a call confirming that she would still be having visitors the next day and would she mind if they brought a third person. Slamming the phone down on the affirmative, she forgot to ask who the third person would be. But, either way, she realised that her attempt at blackmail had not been successful – perhaps the DVD had not arrived in time.

Had she known the third person would be a certain Tom Rendell, she might have been more receptive to the idea of the second visit. As it was, she stormed about the château like someone demented.

Trevor was woken from a deep sleep; he'd had more than enough vino that evening and after a hearty dinner had been glad to get to his hotel bed. The urgent knocking on his door was not at all welcome – who the heck could it be at this hour?

It was Tom and he had a problem. It seemed that when babies want to be born they invariably choose the worst possible moment As in most cases, Tom Junior had unfortunately chosen to make his attempt to join the human race at three in the morning! Tom was full of apologies but the birth of his son had to take precedence over some old paintings. Trevor strongly agreed. The ambulance was called and Cassie and Tom were taken to the nearest hospital, Tom having first suggested that Jessica be asked to accompany Trevor to the château since Paul, who for some reason seemed to have gone to ground, had failed to turn up and Trevor needed a witness to whatever transpired. The only option now was for Trevor to come right out with the knowledge that he did know about the hidden room where the Countess kept the paintings, and if they had to bring Tom and the French police into it then so be it. Finally, he managed to get hold of Paul who apologised, explaining he was delayed in London and authorising Trevor to act on his behalf.

Jessica, who'd had to be told exactly what was going on, was delighted to be involved in a showdown with the rich bitch who had got her talons into Tom. They arrived at the château punctually; they had arranged for it to be after lunch although they accepted glasses of mineral water presented in the usual elegant glass decanter and matching crystal glasses. Trevor was determined that all should go well and that they would get only one response to their visit: Madame Connie would have to come clean about the paintings; whether they were indeed the original Old Masters, where exactly they had come from; and how they had come to be in the Pasteurs' possession.

Cassie was screaming. The pain she had been warned about was even more intense than she could possibly have imagined. Sweat pouring down her face, she writhed about on the hospital bed. The sight of her husband's worried face made her feel only a little better – if she was hurting, she certainly hoped he was too. However, he wasn't, was he? Nothing he was feeling could match the pain she was going through. Damn the man, damn the sex, damn the wedding – damn everything! Her first marriage had been much simpler than this. As for Tom, well he was nice, but bloody hell – he was not worth all this pain. Never again. He could damn well have the snip before he came anywhere near her again; she would insist on it. Cassie, the normally immaculately attired wife of Tom Rendell was not at all composed as she attempted to follow the instructions given first by the midwife then by the apparently unconcerned doctor who had just arrived. Push? What the hell did they think she was doing? If she pushed any harder, the bloody baby would shoot out and end up in the next room. Bathed in sweat, Cassie laboured to bring Tom Junior into the world. It occurred to her in a moment of respite when a contraction came to an end that she could clearly remember the last time she had shed this much sweat – yes, and that was how she had got into this mess in the first place. 'Tom Rendell,' she gasped, 'if you ever lay hands on me again…' but the next contraction followed on the heels of the last and Tom, squeamish and feeling extremely nauseous, never heard what Cassie had intended to say.

Madame Connie showed her visitors into the lounge with its brightly burning fire. The room had an ostentatious air about it. All they had to do was to get Madame Connie to admit to having the paintings. A simple task, surely? In fact it took fifteen minutes before they could get Madame Connie to show them the library. Even then, she just opened the doors to the room and stood back, still insisting that she had no idea what they were on about – secret room indeed! They had clearly been misinformed; it was a cruel joke – or more likely an attempt to malign her.

Trevor waited out the storm of Connie's blustering denials and could see from her defiant expression that, if there was a secret room, he was going to have to find it without her assistance. He had a problem though: he had been told by Tom the approximate location of the book that would open the secret door, but not the title. Tom had stood too far away to see that, but had said it was positioned at about shoulder height because he had seen Connie extending her arm straight out, not raising it or lowering it.

With this in mind, Trevor, with Jessica in tow, walked around the room arriving at the wall which, according to Tom, held the right book. Jessica was the first to locate it. She noticed that, while the rest of the books were in pristine condition, one particular book was rather well worn. Pushing it produced a grinding noise, followed by a door opening to reveal a long narrow room with rows of lights that lit up as you entered. Trevor and Jessica gasped at the splendour of what lay before them. Jessica, more familiar with some of the artists displayed there, walked around the room uttering names of well-known geniuses. When they arrived at the Mona Lisa, they both just stood there – speechless!

Connie watched them, her eyes wet with tears of rage and helplessness. Her secret was out and she now had visions of her precious paintings being moved from their secure resting place and placed into trucks for transportation to God knows where. They belonged to her and to no one else and now, because of her own stupidity in inviting Tom Rendell into her home, she was going to lose them and the wealth they represented. Silently, she began to weep bitter tears of frustration.

Each with their own private thoughts, the three of them continued to stand in the middle of the room gazing up at the Mona Lisa. Trevor, for his part, was rather sad that, while they had achieved what they had come for, Madam Connie's beautiful crestfallen face now portrayed great sorrow. He was about to inform her with some reluctance that he would have to contact the French authorities when he was interrupted by a sudden movement behind him.

'I'm sorry, Madame Connie,' Daniel said, edging nervously round the open door, 'but you have some visitors and they insist on seeing you. Err… one of them works for Mr Rendell.'

'What?' Connie gasped, swinging round. 'Don't let them in, Daniel.'

But it was too late. As Daniel was jerked away by an unseen hand, Connie, Trevor and Jessica found they were gazing at the smiling faces of Trish, Jonathan and Giorgio; his smile was the broadest of the three.

'Trish?' Jessica took a step forward. 'What the hell are you doing here? Giorgio? I don't understand…' Her voice shrank to a whisper as she noticed the guns that the two men were pointing at them.

Jonathan spoke first. 'Thank you, Trevor, and you too, Jessica, for showing us where the paintings are hidden.' Still smiling, he addressed Connie. 'Oh sorry, we haven't been introduced – I take it you are Madame Pasteur, Tom's… err, friend?' He sneered. 'A close one as I understand it.' He laughed as Connie's face went white then red as though he had slapped her.

Watching helplessly, Trevor, trained to deal with these situations, could have kicked himself. His Browning HP was back at the hotel. He had not dreamt he would need to carry a firearm today. How could he have been so lax? Was he getting too old for this game? Thinking rapidly, he eyed the two men. The odds were not good, but sooner or later they would get careless and then he could jump and disarm one of them.

As if reading Trevor's thoughts, Giorgio waved his pistol menacingly at the three captives and motioned them to return to the lounge. Their hearts fell as they saw that the château's entire staff, including Anna and now Daniel, were sitting bound and gagged. The scene was set for the largest art heist of the century.

Jessica looked from Jonathan to Trish and their gleeful faces showed just one thing – revenge was sweet! Sick at heart, she eyed Giorgio. The smarmy bastard had set her up; how could she have been so stupid? She must have been blabbing about the paintings on that infamous night that she couldn't remember. And that was odd too. It came to her in a flash that, of course, she had been drugged. It was the only explanation. She looked daggers at Giorgio but he only winked at her and laughed.

The three new captives were bundled to the floor and handcuffed by Jonathan who looked intently at the Countess and felt a rising surge of pleasure as he admired her voluptuous figure. His fantasy was brought up short by Trish hissing in his ear, 'Don't even think about it, chum. There's no time for that!' She was right, of course. Still, it would have been nice to force himself on Madame Pasteur. Judging by what he'd heard, she would probably even have liked it! Jonathan sighed with regret and turned back to the job in hand.

In a Parisian hospital, the screams had ceased and been replaced by the high-pitched crying of the Rendells' newborn son. Peter Tom Rendell had arrived: seven pounds and four ounces and with a healthy pair of lungs. Tom smiled broadly at his now relaxed wife and simply said, 'Thank you, darling... he is lovely!'

Cassie smiled back at her husband and replied, 'You're welcome. He is lovely, isn't he.' All the evil thoughts of the last four hours had gone – forgotten in the euphoria of the new arrival. She realised that her family was now complete and, as she rested her gaze on the two men in her life, knew she had found the inner peace she had been waiting for all these years. Connie Pasteur – eat your heart out, she thought with a lazy smile.

Connie was having a bad day; her precious paintings were being loaded on the truck that had been brought round to the front door. While Trish watched their captives, Giorgio and Jonathan gently carried their priceless cargo to the truck, taking care to place each one into separate compartments which had obviously been made specially for the event. Jonathan had found two smaller paintings they had not bargained for – still, that was no problem; he would put them behind the driver's seat. They were not leaving anything behind. At around three million euros each, they had outwitted that Trevor fellow and Jonathan could just imagine the look on Tom Rendell's face when he heard all about it. He knew the chances of anybody finding their prisoners would be days – even weeks – plenty of time to carry out their plans to escape France and head back to Italy. From there – well, anything was possible: Spain, Cuba, even Russia. Having finished loading the truck, Jonathan returned, took his gun back from Trish and pointed it at the prisoners motioning them to move. They were herded back through the library and into the secret room, now empty of all its valuable contents.

Jonathan leaned over and kissed Connie on the lips. 'Sorry we didn't have more time to get better acquainted,' he drawled. Connie responded by spitting into his face.

Jonathan, fuming, reacted by hitting her hard across the cheek. 'What's wrong with you, woman,' he sneered. 'Can't you take a joke?' Wiping the spittle off his face with one hand, he leaned over her and slowly pressed the cold barrel of his pistol down her dress and into her cleavage.

Connie screamed. Her tormentor laughed and Trevor, struggling with the handcuffs that coupled him to Connie, promised himself one thing: he would get this man if it was the last thing he did. He had never been able to tolerate men who hit women. The bastard would get what was coming to him; of that Trevor was certain.

'Time to go, Jonathan.' Giorgio appeared round the door.

Lifting the gun, Jonathan nodded. At the doorway, he turned back and smiled at Connie. 'Oh, by the way, we are taking a crate of your finest brandy to keep us warm on our journey – you won't be needing it where you lot are going. I guess you will have at least two hours of fresh air. Have fun!' Trevor suddenly realised that their plight was even worse than he had first figured – the secret room must be airtight and, with all the people present, two hours of air might just be an exaggeration.

'Jessica did well selling the property to Giorgio Cassie,' remarked Tom as he cuddled their new son. 'She certainly pulled all the stops out to settle the deal so quickly. Still, I know she can be a hard person to turn down. I wonder if she used more than her personal charm,' he added, laughing.

Cassie, seeing what Tom was driving at, just laughed. 'Not with that one, Tom. Giorgio is gay!'

Tom stared at his wife. 'How do you know that?'

'Well, I've had plenty of time to observe gay men seeing as my brother is one. While you lot were celebrating the sale, I had a long chat with Jessica. She told me all about Giorgio and his company – "Electroco" she said it was called. She said that she woke up next morning and there she was in his bed and she couldn't remember anything at all about how she got there or what had happened. It sounded to me like she'd been drugged – perhaps a date drug or something? Goodness knows why. Maybe Gorgeous Giorgio didn't want her to know he was gay for some reason? I was going to mention it to you – that is, before he arrived.' She smiled, nodding to their newborn son.

Tom frowned, reaching for his mobile. 'That sounds bad, Cass. He might be a conman targeting Jessica – and she's gone to the château instead of me. I think I'd better phone Trevor to see how it's all going.'

'You're not allowed to use a mobile in here.' Cassie pointed at a sign on the wall.

'Never mind that,' he said, punching in Trevor's number, 'this could be an emergency.' Ten minutes later, he gave up trying as Trevor's mobile went unanswered.

Trevor had examined the room thoroughly but, as Connie had confirmed, there was no way out and the air was limited. The normal procedure was for fresh air to be piped in just once a week to keep the pictures in good order. For the same reason, the temperature was controlled which was why it felt so cool despite the number of people. The possibility of anyone being shut in there had not been taken into account when it was built and nobody had ever stayed in the room to sit and admire the paintings for any length of time. The chances were they would all suffocate eventually. Already they were beginning to suffer from a shortage of air.

Thanking Trevor's foresight in giving him Paul's emergency number, Tom eventually got through to Trevor's boss, explained what had happened and that he had been tied up with the birth of his son.

After a moment's hesitation and sounding extremely surprised to get the call, Paul asked after Cassie.

'Yes thanks, Paul, mother and baby are doing fine... but I'm really worried about Trevor. He's not answering his phone and that's unusual for him. I mean, he always answers, doesn't he?'

'Usually, unless of course he's in an area that limits his connection,' Paul offered.

'Never had any problem when I was there,' replied Tom,

quickly passing over in his mind the events that had taken place while he was at the château. 'Look, Paul, do me a favour – can you quickly check out a company for me and the name of the Deputy Manager, Giorgio something. I don't know his other name, but I think he might be a conman. The company's called "Electroco" but I have a feeling that something is wrong and Trevor and Jessica might be in some kind of danger.'

'Of course, I'll get onto it straightaway,' Paul said crisply. 'I'll call you back.'

He was back within ten minutes. There was no registered company of that name, and needless to say, no 'Giorgio' on record. It looked like Tom's hunch was correct. Tom groaned to himself – he did not wish to worry Cassie so made light of it. She was looking very sleepy and, since she was staying overnight in the hospital, he kissed his son's tiny head, hugged his wife and excused himself, promising to be back in the morning.

He drove quickly towards the château. What he might find there worried him and, as he drove, he made one more call – back to Paul to keep him in the picture and ask him to contact the French police.

Trevor and the rest of the inhabitants in the secret room were now feeling light-headed, a sure sign of lack of air. He tried to give some assurances to everyone – after all he was the G-Man, not that any of them knew it – he must come up with something, but his wrists were securely cuffed and he could see no way out of this situation Connie seemed the worst affected: her face was flushed, the bruise where Jonathan had hit her standing out on her cheek. In the past, Trevor had envied his friend's lifestyle somewhat, but right now he would give anything just to be back in Windsor with his wife and children. Dragging his mind back to the present with some difficulty, Trevor advised his fellow captives to take their time breathing, but his words were slurred and as his thoughts began to dim he knew that how long they would be able to do that was anybody's guess.

Tom was driving as fast as he could towards the château. He was soon joined by the French Gendarmerie who had been alerted by Paul via Interpol. The cars screeched to a stop outside the château and, finding the doors open, Tom and the police ran into the grand hall. The sight that greeted them filled Tom with great relief. Sitting in the lounge, trying to get their breath back, was his friend Trevor and his two ex-lovers, Jessica and Connie, accompanied by all the staff.

Chapter Twenty-Nine

Had things gone to plan, Arthur Thomas would have been celebrating his conquest of the virginal Susan. As it was, he had arrived at the château just in time to see the paintings being loaded onto the truck and straightaway had realised something was wrong – for one thing there was no Daniel or Anna to give him a ticking off for being late. Arthur, not knowing how many villains were involved, had decided to hide behind the bushes and wait and see what happened. He watched three people come out of the front door with two paintings which one of the men inserted behind the driver's seat. Apparently without a fear in the world, they closed the front door of the château, jumped into the truck and made their exit from the grounds. Arthur had let himself in but had difficulty in finding anyone. He knew they had to be somewhere, no one was scheduled for any time off – the Countess only let one person at a time have a day off and last night had been his turn. Walking into the library, he found no one. Where had the staff got to? He returned to the hall and walked upstairs; if he could find the Countess he knew she would certainly know where everybody was. Still no one.

Pictures – he had seen pictures being loaded into the truck, but where had they come from? He could not see any new empty spaces on the walls, so where had they come from? He returned again to the lounge and switched on the overhead light. Suddenly he saw, hastily scrawled in lipstick on the glass coffee table, the word 'Libra'. Arthur Thomas scratched his head; he knew something bad had taken place that evening and that it involved paintings, but where had they come from? 'Libra' must mean library – nothing else tied up. He went back into the library and, making as much noise as possible, started calling out Daniel's and Anna's names. In the secret room, Trevor roused himself; he thought he could hear someone calling Anna's name. Shaking his head, he called out to the others to rouse themselves and started banging on the inside of the door. He managed to get Connie to her feet and she joined Trevor banging hard on the door.

Arthur stopped; he could definitely hear a banging noise. It seemed to be coming from the bookcase and he knocked back, hoping that he was answering in the right place. As he paused to listen, he heard a faint cry coming from behind the bookcase. It took another very long five minutes as Trevor tried desperately to convey to Arthur Thomas the correct book to push on… this was made harder as AT could only hear muffled tones. Homing in on the sound coming from behind the shelves, he began to push and shove, his large hands spreading randomly against the books. Suddenly there was a click and a door swung open. Wrinkling his nose against the fetid, stale air, Arthur stepped inside to be greeted by Madame Connie who, despite still being handcuffed to Trevor, hugged her young rescuer. Arthur, with the help of the now much relieved Trevor, managed to pull the remaining captives out of further harm's way.

A half-hour later, everyone had come round and was feeling much better. Arthur found himself being kissed and hugged by all the staff, including the men! Trevor Miles shook his hand and called him a 'good fellow' and Connie whispered that he was a hero and she would thank him personally later, when she felt better. God, didn't the woman ever think of anything else?

When the French police come bounding in, Madame Connie's face seemed to light up with joy. Rushing towards the man in the lead, she welcomed him as if he had been the one who had saved their lives. Feeling suddenly neglected, Arthur Thomas stood back and gaped: him being the saviour of the hour hadn't lasted long then. And who was this man the Countess was hugging and kissing like there was no tomorrow?

Seeing Arthur's puzzled face, Anna took pity on him. Poor Arthur Thomas; first the farmer's daughter and now his mistress. No wonder he looked so crestfallen. Hiding her amusement, Anna approached him and whispered in his ear, 'I will explain later, dear.'

Arthur nodded absently; his expression said it all: what does a guy have to do to have a reasonable relationship?

Trish, Jonathan and Giorgio had made their escape, driving over the French border and into Italy where Jonathan had plenty of contacts and could hide the paintings. Unloading them into safe and secure storage was easy but, as he took out the last two from behind the driver's seat, Jonathan looked at them and immediately wondered what they would fetch. He had arranged with Giorgio, whose real name was Pearce, for them to stay in his safe house before they tried to dispose of the paintings. The plan was to sell them in Russia or America or even Europe. Private investors were the favourite option; Jonathan had realised that the Vatican would certainly not have any further dealings with him after the last happenings.

Six weeks had passed and soon Pearce started pestering Jonathan for cash; he had expensive tastes and needed money to entertain some of his men friends – after all, he pointed out, Jonathan had Trish to take care of his sexual needs.

Jonathan looked at him. 'Well, Pearce, I'm not a bottomless pit. You can have a couple of hundred euros which will be deducted from your share when it is safe for us to sell the pictures, but you will have to try to suppress some of your urgent urges!' He smirked as he said this which only made the irate Peace even more upset. Pearce continued with his nightly visits to the gay clubs, and the requests for even more cash became more frequent.

In the end, after constant pleading from Pearce, Jonathan decided it would be worth the risk to approach Louis and ask him what he thought of the two smaller paintings. He for one did not know their worth and had not known either of them. He could not, of course, approach Louis himself as he would be recognised and Jonathan did not wish to be forced to leave Italy. They agreed that Pearce would make the approach as an art lover in desperate straits with little knowledge of what the paintings were and how much they could possibly be worth.

Fortunately, Louis always kept his name listed in the local telephone directory as an art dealer, so it was easy to find his number and make the initial approach. Giving a false name, Pearce made the call and it was arranged that he would meet Louis at his office.

Arriving at the office, Pearce went through his tale of woe; the paintings had been left to him by a relative and he needed money quite badly, so what could Louis recommend?

Louis looked at the two paintings before him, stood up and simply replied, 'Nothing, I can see no real value from either of these they are certainly not from any artist I know and the subject is poor – sorry, the best you can do is enter them in a local auction and see if they catch someone's eye.'

Disappointed, Pearce thanked Louis and returned to tell Jonathan the results. Jonathan was immediately enraged; how could this happen? All the other paintings must be of some considerable value so why were these the last two useless? The two men decided there was nothing else for it but to do as Louis suggested and, using an associate of Pearce's, arranged for the two pictures to be put up for auction – at least they should get a bit of cash to help pay their way.

Tom, Cassie and the new baby had now returned to England with Trevor who had invited his friend and newly increased family to stay. Allison, who was feeling increasingly broody, was delighted to have a baby around again, and Cassie fell in love with their large house so much so that Tom decided to sell his small apartment and look around for a new, much larger house for them. This kept him busy while Cassie attended to their son.

Three months later, he found what he wanted and they moved into a new house just a short distance from Trevor and Allison. This made Cassie and Allison happy as it meant they could continue to socialise. The two women quickly formed a close relationship and in due course it was very apparent that Allison had forgiven Tom's original betrayal of her friend Trish; not that Allison now chose to call Trish her friend. Recent events had put paid to that.

As the weeks went by, Tom became increasingly bored and was often heard to mutter, 'Ugh! Too much small talk…' He was only interested in selling houses and making money. This unfortunately was proving rather hard due to the world recession.

Trevor for his part was feeling disappointed that they had been hoodwinked by Jonathan and Trish and could never quite understand why his boss had stepped back from the investigation.

Paul, thankful that his dalliance with the Countess had never come to light, wanted to forget that part of the proceedings but, now and again, he could not help reflecting that he had enjoyed every minute of it. He put the DVD into a safe deposit box. Why, he was not sure; perhaps to remind himself that all that glitters is not gold? Or maybe because he might one day want to watch it again to relive the moment! It was not like these unusual experiences came to him every day!

Interpol routinely sent out the descriptions of all the stolen paintings – something that pleased Connie. She was incensed about losing them and anything that could be done to recover them was better than doing nothing. Of course, she would worry about explaining the basic problem of ownership when it came to it, but possession was still nine-tenths of the law.

The months rolled on and there was still no sign of the stolen paintings. Tom had put the whole business to the back of his mind. He and Cassie took their small son to Rome to visit some of Cassie's relatives and one day, while out shopping, they bumped into Louis.

'I'm pleased that I ran into you, Tom, because I had meant to call you and Trevor, but I've been so busy tied up with extra work, I didn't get around to it.'

'About what, Louis?' Tom asked as they strolled together along the pavement.

'You know the list of stolen paintings that was circulated a few months back? Well, I've seen two of them.'

Tom grabbed Louis by the arm. 'Go on, Louis, when and where! When and where? Tell me.'

Cassie excused herself and left them to it – she for one had

had enough of stolen paintings and the Countess who went with them; she wanted to leave everything well enough alone. 'I'll see you later.' She smiled at her husband and disappeared into an adjacent clothes shop.

Tom groaned and patted his wallet pocket. 'Oh Lord,' he grinned at Louis, 'that's going to cost me. But go on, Louis, you were saying?'

Women, eh! Louis returned a sympathetic grin. 'Well anyway, I had this smooth character come to see if I would be interested in selling two small paintings for him – he had been left them by a relative, he said. They were not of any interest to me and I told him so and suggested that he just placed them in an auction to get what he could for them.'

'Did he do as you suggested, do you know?'

Louis nodded. 'They were listed in the catalogue for last month's auction at the Plaza's auction rooms. I don't know if they actually sold, but it was only then that I remembered the description of the paintings on the list that was sent round.'

'Can you come with me to the auction rooms to see if they sold at all?' Tom asked eagerly, adding, 'And if so, perhaps who bought them?'

'Sure,' Louis agreed, 'it's the least I can do. I should have been more alert about all this – I must have been asleep all that week!'

Hiding his irritation, Tom smiled, but deep down he knew they had all missed the chance of getting on the tail of Jonathan and his gang.

Chapter Thirty

Julio, the owner of the auction room and a long-time friend of Louis', was very helpful. 'Yes, they finally sold at the second attempt to a local dealer by the name of Dante,' he told them. 'I happened to see them in his shop window the other day. I can't tell you off the top of my head what they went for, but I seem to remember they didn't sell very well. I could look it up for you if you're interested…'

'No need,' Tom said.

'Well, if you're thinking of buying them, take my advice and don't pay too much.' Julio grinned.

Tom and Louis went straight to the dealer's shop located just a few blocks from the auction rooms. Sitting surrounded by some impressive works of art in the window were the two paintings in question. It appeared the art dealer wanted to give the impression that they were at least as important as the others he was trying to sell. 'Crafty sod!' Louis muttered as they walked into the shop.

'How much for the pair?' Tom enquired of the price, schooling his expression to one of studied nonchalance.

The dealer's face brightened. 'Well, sir, they are two quite special paintings – ' He cut himself short when he suddenly recognised Louis. 'Oh, hello, Louis, I didn't see you standing there.' Turning back to Tom, he shrugged. 'If you're interested, you can have them for three hundred euros for the two.'

'How about two hundred and fifty for cash?'

'Done!' Dante lifted the pictures from the window and proceeded to wrap them. 'I'll never be able to retire at this rate,' he grumbled, winking at Louis who grinned back.

Tom paid the money and the two men left with the paintings. Later, sitting in the square drinking a couple of local beers, the two men discussed why two very ordinary paintings should come to be tucked away in Connie's secret room with others that could be worth millions – it did not make sense. Getting out his eyeglass, Louis again examined the paintings. 'You know, Tom,' he said after a moment, 'that particular week I must have been brain dead! These could actually be quite good.'

'Eh? What do you mean? I thought they were worthless.'

Tucking his glass back into his pocket, Louis smiled at his companion's baffled expression. 'The thing is, Tom, in the last war it was common practice for owners to hide their precious paintings under other paintings; they painted over them to make them look worthless.'

Tom's eyes widened. 'Are you saying these two paintings could have masterpieces underneath them?'

Gesticulating at Tom in his excitement, his beer slopping onto the table, Louis said, 'I think so, but I can't say for sure. We would have to take them to an expert to get them X-rayed and then have the top layer removed which would take some time, but it's the only thing that makes sense, knowing what we do about the other paintings that were in the secret room.'

Tom then turned his attention to the mystery seller. 'Who was he, Louis, any idea?'

'No idea at all. He didn't leave a card and I've forgotten his name.'

'How did he contact you in the first place?'

'By telephone and of course he didn't leave a number.'

'Not to worry, if you can remember the day he visited you the police might be able to trace the call if he made it by mobile. I'll get onto Trevor; he and Paul should be able to arrange this. We could be on the way to recovering all the paintings, Louis – that is, if Jonathan and his partners in crime have not flown the coop already!'

Trevor was having a meeting with Paul when the call came in. He picked up the phone and mouthed 'It's Tom' at his boss who waited expectantly as Trevor took the call.

'OK, Tom,' Trevor said after a moment, 'give us the date of the meeting and leave it with us.' He ended the call and turned back to his boss. 'We need to find out a phone number – Tom has recovered two of the missing paintings.'

'Has he indeed. Which ones?'

'Don't know – two small ones, which someone tried to sell to Louis of all people. He hasn't got their number but thinks we might be able to trace the call.'

Paul's eyes gleamed; he sat forward in his chair. 'I think we can make time to chase this one up ourselves, Trevor, and at the same time enjoy some of that Mediterranean sunshine.' He smiled. 'It's getting cold again over here...'

Trevor grinned back at him. 'You'll not get any argument from me!'

Still in Italy, Jonathan was sitting with Trish drinking a glass of wine. He was depressed. Trish had been giving him some tongue pie about having to stay cooped up in the cottage they had rented from a friend of Pearce's. They were, of course, unwilling to be seen around the normal places in Rome, but Pearce did not seem to worry; he was out drinking and coming in at all hours of the night, enjoying himself as he had always done. Jonathan, irritated by Pearce's behaviour, had been disappointed when he received the pittance from the auction room via an intermediate friend of Pearce's, which made the amount even smaller. Thinking about it now, he mused, 'I can't help thinking we made a big mistake getting rid of those two smaller paintings.'

Trish looked at him with some disdain. 'Why? What do you mean? I am getting fed up with this. We apparently have millions tied up with all these paintings and yet we're forced to live like pigs! Why can't we go on to Cuba like we planned?'

Jonathan glared at her. 'For Christ's sake, stop grumbling, Trish. You knew we'd have to lie low for a while and, anyway, it's too late to make a run for it now – we should have done that months ago. I was a fool to listen to Pearce, him pestering me for money all the time; he knew we couldn't move the paintings quickly without losing a lot of cash. What I don't understand is why those two were so… oh, my God!' Jonathan groaned, slamming his fist onto his knee.

'What's the matter now?'

'I've just realised what we've done – we have just given away a couple of cover jobs.'

Startled, Trish frowned. 'A couple of what?'

'Cover jobs – the Jews used to get someone to paint over their better paintings in an attempt to dupe the Nazis into thinking they were not worth taking. It didn't always work, of course, and perhaps in this case whoever stole the paintings was not fooled and took them anyway – most likely shot one or two of the family at the same time.'

Trish screwed her face up. 'Did they actually do that?'

Jonathan nodded, a sorrowful look on his face showing for the first time that perhaps he was not quite the ass she was starting to think he was. 'You'll just have to visit whoever bought the pictures and buy them back,' she said.

Later that day, having been informed by the auctioneer of the name of the art dealer who had purchased the two pictures, Jonathan and Pearce arrived at the art dealer's shop to be met with disappointment: the paintings had just been sold to an Englishman.

'Do you know who he was?' Jonathan asked anxiously.

'No,' replied the dealer, 'but he was with Louis Diamond, a well-known local art dealer. I can give you a contact number for him if you like?'

'No thanks.' Grabbing Pearce's arm, Jonathan turned and almost ran out of the shop. Once outside, he cursed roundly. 'That bloody Louis has double-crossed us! He must have known what the pictures were worth and arranged to buy them back for himself.'

Pearce was incensed. 'Do you know where to find him?'

'Yes, but if he knows I'm back he could panic and call the police.'

Pearce looked blankly at Jonathan. 'Well, we must make sure he doesn't get that chance, mustn't we.' He grinned, moving his finger suggestively across his throat.

Jonathan was concerned. 'Look, Pearce, we don't want any trouble. You can't just go around murdering people; it's one thing taking a few paintings but quite another killing someone.'

'We already did if you remember. We left those people at the château to die, so we'll get life anyway.' Pearce shrugged, 'Might as well be hung for a sheep as a lamb.'

'According to the newspaper they escaped.'

'So? That doesn't put us in the clear – besides, taking something of great value is just as bad as knocking someone off.'

Jonathan nodded, his face creased with anxiety. 'I'm still

against hurting Louis though – he might come in useful if we make it worth his while.'

Pearce nodded reluctantly. 'OK, we'll go easy on him. He might not recognise me, but you will have to stay out of sight or our cover will be blown.'

Trevor paced up and down in Paul's office, his face flushed with anger. 'I don't believe it – how could they rule like that?'

'Well, they have and we've been told to toe the line,' Paul said.

'How could they even think about giving all the paintings back to Connie Pasteur – if we do ever get them back – I mean, they were stolen in the first place!' Incensed, Trevor went on, 'And what's this about having to keep her informed at all times on how we are progressing with the investigation? It's a nonsense.'

Paul nodded. 'I agree with what you say but, whether we like it or not, we do have to comply with what the European Parliament has ruled. Until we prove otherwise, the Countess is still the legal owner of all the paintings and we have a duty to retrieve them for her. It appears that Madame Pasteur has some very important friends in extremely high places. What's more, we could in fact be accused of negligence for allowing Jonathan and his gang to steal them – not to mention the part one of Tom's staff played in all this. It might have been avoided if we'd straightaway told Interpol what we knew, whether or not Tom told you in confidence.'

'You'll be telling me next that we have infringed Madame Pasteur's human rights!'

His gaze sliding away from Trevor's angry stare, Paul fiddled with his pen. 'Yes, well, I was coming to that.'

'Oh, my God!' exclaimed the fuming Trevor.

'You'd better contact her and inform her that we've traced the phone call and that it came from the North Italy area, around the Great Lakes. And stop sulking, Trevor – there's nothing we can do about it.'

Trevor retreated from the office shaking his head; he could strangle that Frenchwoman. His mouth twisted in a wry grimace, but then he guessed that would be against her human rights.

Chapter Thirty-One

'Come on, AT, put the last trunk on the roof rack and tell the others to get their fingers out or we'll miss the sun.' Madam Connie Pasteur was beginning to get her sense of humour back, primarily because the EU Parliament had decided to grant her full ownership of all her paintings – once they had been recovered. And what was even better, that Trevor fellow had to comply with their ruling and work non-stop to recover them for her. As for Paul? Well, he had to do it anyway; he had too much to lose if the DVD ever saw the light of day.

Connie smiled to herself as she got into the back seat of her Silver Cloud Rolls Royce, another heirloom of her ex-husband's estate. They don't make them like this any more, she thought as she checked that her speak-easy intercom was still working. It was, which meant she could keep in close contact with Arthur Thomas as they sped along the lanes and highways to the summer holiday villa which the Countess had rented for the next four months. It was her way of rewarding the staff of the château for their support and the discomfort they had endured at the hands of that Jonathan fellow and his gang. It also, of course, gave her two other opportunities: the first to stave off the possibility that her staff would sue her for endangering them at their workplace, and second, it meant she would be in the right area to start looking for her stolen paintings; the possible location having been reluctantly supplied by Her Majesty's Secret Service. She laughed as she thought of Trevor choking on his morning crumpets or whatever he had for his breakfast. He was not her kind of man, maybe because he was too married!

The Countess, with her staff following in a second car, finally arrived at the spacious villa, its swimming pool sparkling invitingly in the sunshine. Set in twenty acres of gorgeous Tuscany countryside, the villa was secluded to say the least. In an even better mood at the sight of it, Madame Connie told her staff to get settled in and that, after serving her evening meal, they could have the evening off and all the next day. Not so Arthur Thomas, however. 'AT,' the Countess said, 'I will need you tomorrow so please get an early night as we'll be setting off early in the morning.'

Arthur Thomas was surprised not to have been asked to her bedroom as he had been several times over the last few weeks – ever since he had rescued everyone from the sealed room. He had enjoyed the rough play that his mistress had forced on him and, while he still regretted not getting to first base with his girlfriend Susan, he had to admit that possibly he might not have been able to manage both of them at the same time. Susan, of course, was an unknown quantity. He looked forward to having the pleasure of finding out more in the not too distant future, that is, if he could get past her manic gatekeeper father.

On the outskirts of Torbole, a small village in Tuscany, Hans and Greta Geist were sitting in their office worrying over their finances; their problem being that they were spending more money than they were getting in. To make matters worse, the difference was immense and they both knew their so-called detective agency was extremely close to going out of business. The knock on their door was answered by Greta who looked up at the tall, young man standing there and waited for him to speak.

'My mistress, Countess Connie Pasteur, doesn't have an appointment,' Arthur Thomas said, gesturing at the car parked in the road behind him, 'but she wonders if you would be able to see her immediately.'

'Yes, certainly,' replied Greta, her eyes widening when she saw the car was a Rolls. Her eyes opened even wider when the young man merely turned and beckoned. Greta stood back to allow him to walk past her and waited while an attractive woman, with not a hair out of place, emerged from the car and walked gracefully into the office. The young man stood back obediently, but the woman glared in his direction, her face a mask of haughty disapproval. Catching the glance, Greta was not surprised.

Connie was furious: what was wrong with him? How dare he behave in such an offhand manner, not opening the car door for her? He was forgetting who paid his wages and who… but remembering that she was here on business and would have plenty of time to take her sore feelings out on Arthur Thomas later, she turned her attention to the matter in hand.

Upon being shown to a chair, Madame Connie eyed up the two people she had come to see, who were now sitting expectantly behind the desk in front of her. Hans spoke first. 'How can we be of service to you, Countess?'

Connie smiled. 'I am here for a reason, of course, but first I wish to establish that you are both aware of our personal connection.'

Greta's eyebrows shot up as she exchanged glances with Hans who looked equally surprised. How on earth could they have any personal connection with this obviously very rich lady? 'Err, personal connection, Madame…?' Hans's voice tailed away.

Connie, rather enjoying the look of puzzlement on the two faces, went on, 'You are Hans and Greta Geist, brother and sister? Your father has passed away and his father was stationed in Berlin during the last war? Stop me if you disagree.' She waited as the two looked at each other and then nodded. Connie continued, 'You are... trying – for want of a better word – to run this... detective agency. Is that not right? You are wondering how I know so much about you?'

Hans, now completely speechless, just nodded while Greta, a flicker of anger crossing her face, stared at Connie, equally speechless.

Without enlightening them, Connie placed three photographs on the desk before them. They were mug shots of Jonathan, Trish and Pearce. 'I want you to find these three and report back to me. Whatever else you are doing, this must take precedence. Is that understood?'

Nettled, Hans shrugged his shoulders and, ignoring Greta's nudge, said, 'I am not sure we will have the time, Madame. We have a lot on just now – '

He was cut off as the Countess launched into a string of expletives that no lady should even have known about, let alone say them out loud. 'Don't insult my intelligence; you are broke, you have no work and are almost bankrupt. You will now work solely for me and you will be paid well for your services.'

Greta and Hans stared open-mouthed at the virago on the other side of the desk.

Aware that she had perhaps overdone it, Connie softened her approach. 'Look, Hans, your grandfather and my husband's father were very close friends. I know all about your family history and what happened during the last war. My father-in-law performed a service of very great danger for your grandfather, and now it is I who need your help. All

I can tell you is that I need these people to be found without delay and I know that you, Hans,' Connie flashed him a sweet smile, 'are uniquely qualified to do this simple job for me.'

His earlier irritation forgotten, Hans's face lit up with pleasure. Here was a grand lady who seemed to know all about him and was telling him – pleasantly this time – that he was unique and well qualified to solve a case for her. He looked at Greta with a smirk on his face; he had often told his sister that he was the one who knew more about detective work than she.

Greta was not so easily taken in. She had listened to her brother constantly over the last six months while they had been working as a detective agency. She had always agreed to whatever he suggested but, out of earshot, had often muttered to herself that her brother was a complete idiot. Greta instinctively distrusted this Madame Pasteur, but as usual said nothing, merely nodded her agreement.

Looking from one to the other of them, Connie was satisfied. Standing up, she took from her purse a large wad of euro notes and threw them on the desk. Greta reached forward eagerly and picked them up; whatever she felt about this high-handed woman, they would come in useful just now.

'There are two hundred thousand euros there,' Connie said. 'There is no need to count them and when you find these people,' she indicated the three photographs, 'there will be the same amount again. But remember, I do not wish you to mention me in any circumstances; just report back to me when you have found them. Do you understand?'

Hans nodding vigorously, plainly unable to believe his good fortune, cleared his throat and asked lamely, 'Do you, err… have any idea, Madame, where we should start looking?'

Gazing at his eager, sweaty face, Connie wondered if she was placing too much faith in this luckless pair of peasants.

'Perhaps you can start at the Club Serpentine. I would imagine that you might have heard of it?'

Hans's face flushed. 'Well yes, Madame Pasteur, I know it well, but why – '

Impatiently, Connie cut across him. 'I shall be at this number when you find something out.' She flicked her card onto the desk. With that, she flounced out of the office and got into her car. Arthur Thomas, after hearing the last load of obscene language coming from the lips of his lady boss, had decided not to risk pushing his luck by not being there to open the door for her.

When the Rolls had driven away, Greta closed the office door and turned to look at her brother. 'Doesn't the Countess know the Serpentine is a gay club, Hans?'

Hans turned away as if to hide his red face. Looking down at the handsome, slightly effeminate mug shot that grinned up at him from the desk, he now knew why the Countess had said he was 'uniquely' qualified to find the men she sought. She had not being paying him a compliment after all. How could she have known that he was a homosexual? He shuddered; this woman seemed to know everything about them, and it went back to the old days and his father's closely guarded secret: that his own father – Hans's and Greta's grandfather – had worked as an SS Officer in the Third Reich.

Connie smiled to herself as the Rolls made its way back up the hill leading back to the villa. 'Pull up here, AT, this will do nicely. Go ahead and unpack the picnic lunch that Anna made for us. Have a drink yourself.'

Arthur Thomas laid out the rug and set out the contents of the picnic basket; there was wine, plenty of food and the best glasses – the Countess always required the best. Sipping his wine, Arthur looked at the scene before them: the beautiful rolling hills, the clear blue sky that seemed to touch the lush green grass which here and there was broken up by the rich brown and yellow bracken. Yes, this part of Italy was certainly lovely, to say the least, he reflected, thinking about his girlfriend. Perhaps one day he would bring Susan here so they could experience it together. He glanced up at his boss and his heart sank as he noticed the glint in her eye. Oh no, not again, Madame, he thought with a sigh as he found himself being pushed back on the rug, causing him to empty his glass's half-drunk contents all over himself as the bottle of wine tipped over. He should not have worried; he found his shirt being pulled apart and a warm tongue seeking out the cold wet liquid as if in a vain attempt to stop it spilling any further. Arthur knew from past experience what that warm tongue could do in that particular area of his anatomy and he braced himself in anticipation as it pursued the dribbling wine southwards. Madame Connie was taking her own form of retribution – good God! What would she do if he had actually stolen the blessed car?

Anna and Daniel were enjoying the pool, the ambience of the villa made even better by the absence of their demanding mistress. They lay back with the other members of the château staff, soaking up the afternoon sun that seemed to devour their minds leaving their bodies totally relaxed. They had never been able to experience this before; they always seemed to be on call. They also knew that they had a lot to thank Arthur Thomas for: first, saving their lives and second, keeping a smile on Madame's face! If that estate agent Tom could not be there, then the young English chauffeur fitted the bill perfectly.

Daniel reached lazily for the ice bucket. 'More wine, Lady Anna?'

'Certainly, my man,' replied the lady in question; sometimes it was nice to dream...

After an uneventful journey, Trevor and Paul had arrived in Italy and were meeting up with Tom and Cassie, having decided to treat the two to a nice evening meal at their local restaurant. Cassie had arranged for one of her doting relatives to babysit. She had welcomed the chance to dress up, not having managed that too often, she being a full-time mum. The sound of this had a nice ring to Cassie, who revelled in the fact that the dream most girls have from about the age of twelve – to meet someone nice, marry them, and have children – had come true for her.

Gazing lovingly at her handsome husband, Cassie felt a frisson of excitement; he still had that certain something that turned her on. She promised herself that when they got home from the restaurant she would take serious advantage of him. What with the baby wanting constant feeding in those first few months, Cassie had not felt like availing herself of one of her husband's numerous talents, but now... yes, tonight would be something else. Tonight, thought Cassie, I shall be a mother, a wife and a whore... just for tonight!

Tom, completely unaware of his wife's lascivious thoughts was enjoying his friends' company when he suddenly noticed Paul's diamond cufflinks which were identical to his own. Before he could stop himself, he smiled and, indicating his own cufflinks, said, 'Snap!' Taken aback and looking faintly embarrassed, Paul made no comment but Tom, being more au fait with a certain lady's actions and responses, sat thoughtfully back in his chair and proceeded to weigh everything up.

Could he be mistaken? Had the lady spider entrapped one of Her Majesty's secret agents – and a senior one at that – he was Trevor's boss, after all. Tom looked again at the shining cufflinks that glittered in the subdued lighting of the restaurant. They were very distinctive – but then, perhaps it was just a coincidence. Tom supposed they could be bought from any good jeweller. However, as the evening wore on, he could not get the cufflinks out of his mind. He dearly wanted to ask Paul where he had got them, but no, surely it was ridiculous? Even so, he might ask Trevor, when he got him on his own, if his boss had ever been left alone for any amount of time with Madame Connie. That decided, Tom managed to place his suspicion to the back of his mind – for the time being at least.

Paul and Trevor had brought Tom up to date with where they thought the gang of art thieves were and also the decision of the European Union who wanted the pictures returned to the Countess should they ever recover them. Tom just shrugged; he had lost interest in the paintings now that he had been excluded from their sale. Trevor did get his attention back a little when he mentioned that the Countess was putting up a reward of ten million euros for their safe return.

Tom's interest increased; that could buy a lot of properties. He had been toying with the idea of going into rental properties since the property market had collapsed, with many houses now being offered at ridiculously low amounts as owners became increasingly desperate to sell and dropped their prices drastically. Perhaps he should think about it again. The problem would be collecting the reward from Madame Connie herself and that would take some doing; Cassie might have some influence on that! Still, the prospect of pulling off such a feat filled Tom with some exciting thoughts. Shame on you, Tom Rendell, and you a married man. Shame on you.

Chapter Thirty-Two

Trish and Jonathan waited for the return of Pearce who had travelled to Rome to meet up with Louis. Jonathan had given strict instructions to Pearce that he should use just enough force to find out who had purchased the paintings. Pearce returned triumphant: yes, he knew who had bought the paintings... but Jonathan would not like it. The purchaser was Tom Rendell!

Jonathan was beside himself with rage; how could he have been so dumb as to sell the two paintings in the first place, and now, of all people, Tom Rendell had got hold of them. It not help matters finding out that Madame Pasteur had been advertising a ten-million euro reward to anyone recovering her precious paintings. That kind of money would always tempt the many crooks in the art world if they were to find out their real location. The knowledge of this made him even more agitated. Damn the woman!

He knew that he had exposed the fact that they were still in the immediate area; in addition to this, he realised that, by Pearce using the mobile phone, the call could be traced to their address. He could not be sure of that but he decided they should move straightaway and he told the other two of his intentions. Pearce was sent out to find another suitable hideaway. At least he was good for something, Jonathan thought bitterly as Pearce sauntered away.

After several hours of looking around, Pearce had failed

to come up with anything but, given he had not agreed with Jonathan about the need to relocate, his efforts were only half-hearted. He would try again tomorrow, he decided. In the meantime, he would call in at his club and relax for a while before returning to hear Jonathan express his displeasure about him not finding a new abode. He grunted as he reflected that Jonathan was acting more like a wife than a partner – and, what was more, without the sex! Actually, he found Jonathan quite tasteful; if it wasn't for that damn lady friend of his – the big-titted tart – he might've stood a chance.

He was greeted by several of his male friends as he sat down at the bar and ordered a '7-high', his favourite drink of Canadian Club with Seven-Up. He had long been addicted to it; he liked the taste and it made him feel randy. He had just finished his third glass when he became aware that he was being eyed up by a young blond man who was trying to catch his eye. In the past, Pearce had seen this man around the club and had long admired his pert arse but had never spoken with him. Indeed, his own smiles in the blond man's direction had seemingly gone unnoticed and he had felt rebuffed, almost as if the guy thought Pearce was not good enough to take things further. However, today Pearce wondered if his luck was in because here was this extremely good-looking, virile young man apparently coming on to him. Pearce glanced behind if to convince himself that he was indeed the centre of this amazing blond hunk's attention. It appeared that he was and he smiled broadly as the man came over and sat down on the next bar stool.

'Hi there, my name is Hans. Who are you?' His words came easily and his eyes sparkled invitingly. Pearce felt a warm flush and knew his face was colouring up; good God, he didn't want to appear too eager. It was hard not to though, for here was a Greek god with deep blue eyes, a perfect tanned complexion and elegant poise, looking only at him. I'm in love! Pearce thought ecstatically.

It did not take Hans long to guide his new friend out to his car: a red Porsche, which looked brand new. In the car, Pearce sat quietly, his thoughts however running wildly. What was happening? Was he dreaming? He could not believe his luck.

It was not long before they arrived at an extremely elegant building and Pearce found himself being led up to an apartment of a kind he had only dreamt of – a dream that, with the stolen paintings, Pearce knew was now well within his grasp. Either way, he soon found that being the poorer of the two men had its advantages. It gave him some satisfaction to be treated as 'a bit of rough!'

It had been several weeks since the Countess had given her instructions to her new members of staff Hans and Greta. There had been no contact from either of them so she decided to pay yet another visit to the detective agency. Leaving AT outside in the car, she entered the office and was surprised to find Greta there on her own. Questions about her absent brother were met with some degree of indifference and it appeared to Connie that neither Greta nor Hans were too interested in solving the task she had asked them to do. Her temper rising, Connie glared at Greta: how dare this insolent girl stare back at her with such belligerence; didn't she know she ate girls like her for dinner – every day!

Connie decided enough was enough and, walking towards Greta, started to launch into her usual torrent of abuse. These were cut short as Greta suddenly lunged round the desk, grasped Connie's face and kissed her fully on the lips. Relaxing her grip a little, she whispered, 'If you have nothing nice to say – don't say anything at all.'

Speechless for once, Connie shrank back in horror. What was the girl doing – but then she allowed her to do it all over again. For once, Madame Connie Pasteur, vamp of the underlings, had met her match.

Trevor by now had been advised by Tom of certain similarities in the cufflinks that he had previously shown to his friend and those that were now securing Paul's shirt cuffs. Trevor could not believe it. There had to be a perfectly simple explanation as to why his rather pompous boss was now attired with such glittering diamond cufflinks. They had to be worth thousands of euros – surely out of the range of even one of Her Majesty's top G Men? Trevor was not by any means a vindictive man and his boss had always treated him with great respect. It was none of his business what Paul got up to in his spare time, but well, damn it – a man's got to do what a man's got to do – Trevor knew he would not be able to resist mentioning the cufflinks to Paul when he had the chance. It would, however, be several weeks before that happened. Swept along by events, both he and Paul were to find themselves tied up with much more pressing things.

'I'm fed up waiting for Pearce to sort things out!' Trish shouted at Jonathan. He groaned, hearing yet another barrage of despairing remarks from his girlfriend. Good grief, he had just about had enough of her – always moaning about everything, even their lovemaking had fizzled out; not at all passionate like it used to be. Yes, as far as Jonathan was concerned, if he could get rid of this woman, he would. The only thing left for him to do was to dispose of some of the paintings so he could pay both her and Pearce off. The problem was – sell them to whom? Everyone in the art world, including Louis, must know about the theft and they would be too worried about taking receipt of them without having a buyer straightaway. Jonathan also knew he would only get a fraction of their true value and, having sold the others for such a good price – admittedly to the Vatican – didn't make it any easier. The initial amount of commission he had received had just about gone now and, with Trish constantly moaning, he knew he had to do something and do it fast! He forced himself to concentrate on identifying a potential buyer and eventually came up with a name from his past: Giovanni Skaletie. Neglecting to inform Trish where he was going, Jonathan set off to track him down.

Giovanni was a farmer who loved to dabble in antiques. He had a small farm just outside Rome and had made his money mainly from selling farmland for development when he was able to grease the hands of people in the right places, i.e. the local authorities. Jonathan had met him several years before when he had accompanied his father whom Giovanni had called out to ask him to buy an old painting from him. Jonathan's father had given him a good price and the two men had become friends, so it was not too difficult for Jonathan to contact Giovanni and put a proposition to him. How would he like to earn some money and be a hero at the same time?

Confused, at first the old man took some time to recognise Jonathan, but then nodded. Times were incredibly hard and he had not been able to sell anything other than a few cows and sheep. What was the deal?

Jonathan's plan was simple: Giovanni would discover the paintings in one of his old barns – contact Madame Connie and claim the reward. Jonathan and Pearce would pay him off and everyone would be happy. A share of ten million euros would be most welcome – the best part being that when Connie arrived to collect the paintings she would find some of them missing, such as the Mona Lisa, which Jonathan intended to keep for himself. He reasoned that she would still be obliged to pay the ten million or lose face. Giovanni could put on his old man act and profess ignorance as to how the paintings came to be in his barn.

Giovanni appeared hesitant at first but, after being reassured that as far as his part was concerned all he had to do was to call the number listed on the reward poster and the rest would follow, he agreed. Jonathan said he would sort things out and be back within two days with the paintings.

Pearce by now was dating heavily. He had been staying over at his new friend's apartment and, upon hearing that he could at last be in for some reasonable money, agreed to go along with the 'found picture' scam. He wanted desperately to treat Hans; after all he had to hold his end up somehow.

Hans had listened intently to his lover's boasting of all the wealth he was about to inherit and how he would repay Hans's kindness ten times over! It did not take long for Hans to discover that Pearce's new found wealth was going to occur in the next twenty-four hours. That night, Hans took Pearce to his bed early and plied him with the usual drinks which he knew would soften Pearce's tongue.

Pearce awoke with a headache – what the heck had he been drinking? Hans seemed fine – but being half German, perhaps drinking schnapps, his national drink, had left him reasonably sober.

'Stay, rest up, Pearce darling,' Hans suggested to his lover. 'You just need some rest – been over doing it just a bit, dear?'

Pearce shook his head. 'No, I must go. I have to help Jonathan with some moving today.' It pleased him that Hans suddenly looked very concerned. 'Don't worry about me.'

Pearce managed a wan smile. 'I'll be OK.'

'Look, I guess we should not have had that last bottle of schnapps – my fault, I did insist. Why don't you let me drive you to wherever you have to go? I'll wait in the car while you do what you have to do and then we can return home and I will give you a soothing massage, my darling.'

Pearce perked up. 'That would be nice.' He pictured himself on the large bed, Hans's soft, manicured hands gently massaging cooling lotion in all the right places. 'Sounds good to me,' he murmured, lying back and idly watching Hans slide out of bed and disappear into the en suite.

'How far are we headed?' the ever obliging Hans called from the bathroom as he quietly dialled a number on his mobile phone.

Pearce's shouted instructions were quickly recorded by Arthur Thomas seated in the Rolls around the corner from Hans's apartment. While she waited, Connie smiled to herself, remembering in detail last evening's amazing love-in with her new found friend, Greta. She had never tried it with a woman before – it simply would never have occurred to her that a woman could satisfy her appetite. How wrong she had been! Tom Rendell, eat your heart out.

With the pictures in the van, Jonathan arrived at the farm and was not at all pleased to see Pearce apparently being dropped off by a man who insisted on kissing him brazenly on the lips. Feeling a little uncomfortable, Jonathan watched as the man retreated to his car, apparently content to wait while Pearce went about his work.

'Let's get on with it, then,' Jonathan grunted, ignoring Pearce's sudden grin. They removed all the paintings from the van and piled them carefully in the old barn which the farmer had cleared out for them, leaving enough covering fodder to make it look as if someone had hidden them securely. Both men were happy with their morning's work and, smiling, gave Giovanni one of the posters indicating that a reward of ten million euros was being offered upon the safe return of the paintings.

The smile on Jonathan's face broadened as he realised that Pearce, in his rush to finish the job and get back to his lover, did not appear to miss the two paintings that Jonathan had kept back as a reasonable amount of extra commission for himself. Reasonable amount! Not bad if you think thirty million euros reasonable, he thought to himself – no wonder the lady in the picture had such an enigmatic smile!

Connie could not believe her luck. They had envisaged some trouble in obtaining the pictures but, observing that Jonathan and company were simply driving away with the farmer to make the phone call, well, it was just incredible. Goodness – first a new lover and now all her precious pictures returned in the space of a week. Connie herself took the call from Giovanni on her mobile phone, letting out a shout of apparent glee as the farmer explained that he had discovered some old pictures hidden in his barn. Could they be ... er... her missing paintings? He could not be sure, of course, as he was only a farmer, not an art expert. Connie quickly arranged to go there the next day when she had organised some transport – fortunately, she was staying in Italy so it would not be long before she could be at the farm. How fortunate was that?

The following day, she arrived at the farm promptly at twelve noon, the pre-arranged time. Giovanni eagerly ushered her and Arthur Thomas into the barn. He led the way to the spot where he had 'discovered' the paintings and pulled back the bales of hay that had allegedly hidden the cache from view.

His face showed total disbelief. He scrambled about, moving them from one position to another and gabbling, 'But they were here, Madame, I swear they were.' It took twenty minutes before Connie, feeling rather sorry for the poor farmer, gently patted him on his arm and suggested that perhaps he should stop drinking so much and maybe have an afternoon nap. No, it was alright bringing her all the way here on a wild goose chase. After all she was a reasonable person – wasn't that right, AT?

Arthur Thomas nodded, hoping that his face did not betray the real thoughts that were running through his head. 'Yes, of course,' he lied, 'she is one of the nicest, most considerate people you could ever meet!'

Chapter Thirty-Three

In the cottage he now shared exclusively with Trish since Pearce had moved in with his gay lover, Jonathan waited patiently to receive the phone call from Giovanni, the call that would result in the gang receiving the ten-million euro reward. Soon, he thought, congratulating himself on coming up with such a foolproof plan, all their troubles would be over.

Pearce had gone back to the apartment with Hans and was receiving his promised massage. He lay soaking up the attention being lavished on him and felt great; not only was he soon to receive his considerable share of the reward money, but here he was having the best rub down he could remember. Life was certainly sweet. Drifting into a pleasurable doze, he heard Hans say something.

'What was that, Hans? Can I trust Jonathan? Of course I can, we've been through a lot together. It's true we did originally envisage receiving much more for the paintings, but that's not Jonathan's fault. We will just have to make do with a mere five million euros each.' He grinned. 'Less a few thousand to the farmer.' He put on a pained expression; then laughing said, 'I guess we'll have to put up with that!'

Finishing the massage, Hans looked down at the smirking Pearce. 'I guess you're right, Pearce darling, just so long as Jonathan has not gone back and taken the paintings – again. I mean, how would you know?'

His eyes narrowed, Pearce thought for a moment then shrugged his shoulders. 'Nah – too much hassle, we had too many problems getting rid of them in the first place – no, having five million each is much better than none.' These words were only just out of Pearce's mouth when the phone rang. Smiling, he reached for it. 'That'll be Jonathan now.'

At first he could not take in what Jonathan was relating to him: the pictures they had secreted in the barn had gone missing – apparently, before Madame Connie had arrived to retrieve them, all the paintings had been stolen again.

Pearce was beside himself – how could that happen? Before he had a chance to scream down the phone, his partner in crime had rung off. Shaking with anger, his face red, he looked helplessly at his gay lover who, unlike Jonathan, would never let him down and said, 'I've been completely screwed, Hans. You were right to suspect Jonathan. The whole claiming the reward thing was obviously an elaborate plan to do me out of my share!'

Nodding sympathetically, his face a picture of concern, Hans watched as the incensed Pearce flung on some clothes, kissed him goodbye and rushed from the apartment. Getting into his car, he sped back to the cottage. There was only one thing on his mind and that was to sort Jonathan out once and for all.

Jonathan was trying to explain to Trish that what had happened was a mystery to him and he had no idea where the pictures had gone when he heard a car screech to a stop outside the cottage. He turned around just in time to see Pearce leap out of his car, aim a gun at him and pull the trigger. He did not hear the gun being fired but felt a searing pain as the bullet entered his chest with such force that it spun him round causing him to fall to the ground. He was aware of Trish screaming and crying out as he lost consciousness.

It was Trish's turn to be on the receiving end as Pearce, now completely out of control, shouted, 'You must have been in on it – you bitch!' Trish was not as lucky as her partner Jonathan; the bullet entered directly into her heart and she dropped like a stone, a look of terror frozen forever on her pretty face. Trish, the housewife turned thief, had now paid a horrible and final price for her involvement in a simple art theft that, for her – a woman scorned – had been only for revenge.

Coming to his senses, Pearce stared down at his victims; they must both be dead. Trish was; he could see by the frozen stare of her eyes, and Jonathan, well he had dropped where he had been shot and, judging by the blood which was oozing from beneath his body, also had to be dead. The one last thing Pearce knew he had to do before he left the scene was to raise Jonathan's right hand and, after wiping his own fingerprints off the gun, place it in the dead man's grasp – a lover's tiff; what could be better than that?

Feeling sick, Pearce arrived back at Hans's apartment and, knocking earnestly on the door, was surprised when it swung open. He hesitated; he knew he would get some comfort from his lover for while he should have listened to him, surely if he admitted that Hans had been right he would be OK about what had happened? Pearce was so sure of that fact that what now faced him was an even greater shock. His face blanched as he pushed the door open wider and walked further into the apartment.

It was almost completely empty – stripped bare – nothing: not a stick of furniture, not even a wine glass. Pieces of Pearce's personal clothing lay scattered about the apartment as if someone had rummaged through everything as if to ascertain the value of each garment. It soon became apparent that nothing was missing which seemed to underline that the person doing this wanted nothing more to do with the dismayed Pearce. Sinking to his knees, he tried desperately to come to terms with what had happened. He had killed his two partners and now he had apparently lost his lover. It appeared that Hans, for whatever reason, had done a bunk. Could anything else possibly go wrong? The sound of authoritative voices at the apartment door answered his question. Pushing himself to his feet, Pearce turned around and was confronted by two policemen who wanted to talk to him about a shooting. Would he mind accompanying them to the police station? No, he didn't have a choice, they told him, escorting him firmly to their car.

He was taken to the local police station and locked away in a cell. He had never felt so down – how could they possibly have made the connection to him so quickly? Surely they could not even have found the bodies yet – he was sure he had not been seen. It made no sense.

The inspector who questioned him was blunt and to the point – if Pearce would come clean now and save a lot of time, it might be possible to treat the killing as a crime of passion – manslaughter carried a much lighter sentence than murder, he added persuasively.

Passion? Pearce thought miserably. Why would this idiot expect him to confess to a crime of passion? After all, he was gay: he would hardly be likely to kill straight men and women over love!

'Don't be silly. I admit I know the two dead people, but I was nowhere near them – I was with my lover, Hans, and we were having a nice relaxing afternoon massaging each other,' Pearce announced easily, feeling suddenly better. Wherever he was, Hans would give him an alibi, he was sure of it.

The inspector pursed his lips, a look of distaste crossing his sombre features. 'Can you remember what time this was, sir?'

'Yes certainly, it was between three and six o'clock today.'

'Are you sure, sir?'

'Of course I'm sure – do you think I'm stupid?'

'Well, sir, if that's the case…' The inspector looked down his nose at Pearce who nodded furiously, 'then I'm afraid we have to arrest you for the murder of Hans Geist who we understand was your live-in lover.'

'What?' Pearce swayed and fell to his knees, almost passing out. This was a nightmare – what was this about his live-in lover? Hans dead? No! It couldn't be true; it had to be a nightmare. 'No, not me,' he kept repeating as they hauled him to his feet. 'And what's this about two other people who apparently have been killed?' The policeman eyed Pearce with a look of contempt. 'You seem to know something about their deaths – whoever and wherever they are. What more can you tell us about this?'

It took another two hours of intensive questioning before Pearce broke down and told the police what they wanted to know. Now totally confused, he could only stare at the inspector and whisper, 'Not me, not me.' His denials made no difference; he was handcuffed and taken to his prison cell. Some hours later he was charged with the murder of Trish Andrews. It transpired that Jonathan Green had survived the shooting and was now recovering in hospital. He had named Pearce as the person who had shot him and his partner. Pearce didn't have a leg to stand on.

Cassie and Tom had returned to the United Kingdom with their son and were spending time again with Allison who had phoned Cassie and asked them to come and stay for a while. Her real motive was to break the news about Trish's death.

'It's all very mysterious,' Cassie remarked to Tom. 'Allison says Trevor asked her to call us as he's away on business in Europe, but he wants to see us urgently as soon as he gets back. She couldn't say why.'

Sitting down with Allison who made a fuss of the baby was a delight for Cassie, but when Trevor arrived home and called Tom out into the garden, she suddenly felt nervous. Whatever was wrong? She looked up just in time to see her husband collapse. Plonking the baby onto Allison's lap, Cassie rushed out into the garden where Trevor told her of the tragic killing of Trish, her one-time friend and colleague. They then had the difficult task of phoning Jessica to inform her of the sad news. All past grievances were put aside as they arranged for Trish's body to be returned to the UK for the funeral. Cassie herself had mixed feelings as she recalled the distressing events that had occurred at the château but the enormity of Trish's sudden murder took over and tears welled in her eyes as comforted her husband who was obviously very upset about his ex-partner's death.

As Jonathan Green signed himself out from the hospital and walked unsteadily to the taxi to make his escape, he for one was glad to smell the fresh air of the Italian countryside.

Arriving back at the château, Madame Connie smiled. 'This will be your room, Greta, when of course you are not visiting me in mine.'

Greta smiled sweetly. 'Connie darling, it's very nice and may I say thank you for giving me a fresh start here in your lovely home. We must, however, arrange for a new headstone for my poor brother – I will always remember his face when I shot him with his own gun, poor dear!'

Chapter Thirty-Four

It was a silent group that returned to Trevor and Allison's house after burying Trish. Cassie and Jessica just could not believe what had happened; even though they knew Trish had been heavily involved with taking the pictures from Madame Connie's château, to be shot and killed in such a tragic manner and by one of her own partners in crime was simply awful. They still could not believe it.

Paul, who had attended the funeral, seemed as shocked as everyone else. He, Trevor and Tom were talking quietly together when Paul received a phone message informing him that a certain Jonathan Green had signed himself out of the hospital and had vanished. Trevor groaned; why hadn't the Italian police placed a guard on him? After all, he was an important witness to the shooting.

'Well, it's not that bad,' Paul explained. 'They do now have a complete confession from Pearce who, seemingly overcome with despair, has put his hands up to both the killings. It won't not be hard to obtain a conviction. As far as Jonathan's concerned however, no one has any idea where he is but I'm sure they'll catch up with him eventually. He'll be brought to book for his part in the robbery, of that you can be sure.'

Connie was now resigned to the fact that she would not be able to place the pictures up for sale again; they were now as hot as the passion she and Greta were enjoying. Arthur Thomas was given the task of restoring the paintings to their respective places in the not-so-secret room, from where they had been removed by the gang.

Connie and Greta were sharing a bottle of Italian wine when he came in and dropped the bombshell: four paintings appeared to be missing. Responding with cries of disbelief, Connie rushed to the room only to find that Arthur Thomas appeared to be correct. There were paintings missing and, even worse, two of them were the most valuable of all – one being the Mona Lisa. How could this be? Surely they had all been there when they took them from the barn? Connie looked sternly at him, almost as if to accuse him of taking or losing them.

Arthur Thomas understood that stare and glared back at the Countess. 'Don't think I had anything to do with it,' he snapped. 'Daniel and I were both present when we retrieved the paintings and we just loaded up what was in the barn. If they aren't here now then they were not in the barn in the first place.'

Connie knew that if Daniel had helped then what AT was stating had to be true. She then wondered if Jonathan had sold or kept back four of the paintings or whether that old farmer had double-crossed her, but how could she find out? The only people who knew for sure would be Jonathan or Pearce. Connie was incensed; she felt cheated and she would not put up with that. Someone would pay for this. Her temper at boiling point, she was on the point of calling Paul to report the theft of the four missing pictures when she suddenly realised that to do that would be to confess that she had hoodwinked the thieves and got the paintings back; and then what? Would they be taken away from her? Thoughtfully, Connie put down the phone and poured herself a large glass of wine.

Back in the UK, the group had said their farewells to Trish and life went on much as before. Tom and Cassie planned to return to Italy, both needing a vacation to recover from the shock of Trish's demise – Tom, with whom she had lived for five years or more, was the hardest hit, and both he and Cassie realized it would be some time before they could truly accept what had happened. For his part, Trevor now had to go back to the old routine of keeping an eye on certain people who were a danger to society. That generally meant many cups of coffee and endless reports, which as usual would land on Paul's desk.

Reading the closing report of the Pasteur case which Trevor had completed that day, Paul began to think further about what had taken place: there were many things that had not been fully explained. The first being: why had the killings taken place at all? They knew that the three must have argued, but to shoot Trish dead and then this fellow Hans did not make sense at all. The copy of the interview with Pearce that had come through from Italy, now conveniently translated into English, was of no help – boy meets boy and kills him in a lover's tiff and then falls out with his partners. 'All nice and straightforward,' Paul murmured to himself, 'except that no one is mentioning the paintings. What happened to them and, more to the point, where are they now?'

Calling Trevor into the office, Paul asked what he was doing at present. 'Not much,' replied Trevor cautiously, sensing that he was about to be sent off to goodness knows where on a difficult assignment which is what usually happened when his boss queried his workload. His instincts were correct:

'I'd like you to return to Italy. There are a few things I believe need to be checked out.'

Trevor could not believe his ears. Back to Italy – perhaps

he could take Allison? Paul smiled but shook his head. No, he wanted Trevor to go and see Pearce who had now been tried, found guilty of murder and given a life sentence

'I'm convinced that not everything has come out about these shootings,' Paul said, 'and what's more, what are they doing about arresting Jonathan for his part in stealing the paintings?'

Trevor nodded; he had been wondering about that himself.

Since Allison, having had several revealing chats with Cassie, had finally put two and two together about her husband's supposed occupation, Trevor had been forced to tell her the complete truth about his secret life as a government G Man. It was a truth she could have done without although, as she had told him, while it meant that she would worry about what he was doing, it did mean he no longer had to lie to her. From Allison's point of view, however, this proposed trip to Italy did look like a nice holiday and, once he had interviewed the convicted murderer, he would, of course, be able to meet up with Tom and Cassie, so she was a bit put out when he said he couldn't take her with him. Realising that he needed to mend some bridges after years of lying to Allison, Trevor again asked and this time received permission from Paul to take his wife and family to Italy with him – with the one proviso that he paid for their trip himself. Nice one, Paul!

Tom and Cassie were thrilled to hear about the Miles family's intended visit and straightaway made arrangements to accommodate them. Cassie and Allison spoke on the phone a few days before their departure, 'At least you'll have some company while the men go off playing cops and robbers.' Cassie giggled.

Tom was only too pleased to accept Trevor's invitation to

accompany him to the prison where Pearce was serving out his life sentence. Would they be able to persuade him to give them any more information that would help them track down Jonathan and the paintings?

Pearce was taken out of his cell and ushered into the interview room where he was confronted with stern looks from Trevor and Tom. Trevor had mixed feelings about meeting the crook again. It did not help matters recalling that the bastard had been happy for him and the château staff to die. For his part, Tom knew he was looking at Trish's killer. Although he was now married to Cassie, Tom had always kept some special feelings for his former partner. The only twist was that at his trial Pearce had insisted that he had not killed Trish, and he certainly had not killed Hans. He maintained his innocence of both the crimes and now said that he had only confessed under extreme pressure from the Italian police; to the point where he would have confessed to anything!

Great, thought Trevor as he sat down and listened to the pathetic prisoner. Pearce wanted to do a deal; he would tell them what had taken place and where he thought the paintings were. Trevor shook his head. No deal. But if Pearce did assist them he would put a word in for him; maybe even get a few years knocked off for good behaviour.

Suspecting this was unlikely, Tom looked sharply at Trevor. However, seeing his friend's expression, he knew instinctively that he was only going through the motions; trying to get out of Pearce the vital information they all needed even if it meant misleading him.

Realising he had limited options, Pearce started relating his story. Yes, he and Jonathan had taken the paintings and put them in a safe place and yes, they had set up the farmer with his tale of finding them in order to get their hands on the reward.

Trevor and Tom exchanged glances and leaned forward in their chairs. 'You mean you actually contacted Madame Connie to inform her that the paintings would be returned to her for a price?' Trevor asked.

Aware that he now had their interest, Pearce replied, 'Yes, for ten million euros.'

Tom then asked, 'Did she agree to pay your farmer friend – which, of course, meant you too?'

Pearce nodded. 'Yes, but when she arrived at the farm the paintings were gone – taken by that rat Jonathan!'

Trevor was not convinced; it seemed too obvious. 'Tell us more about your friend; the one you allegedly killed.'

Pearce's face changed, his angry frown replaced by a wistful smile. 'I did not kill Hans; I was in love with him.'

'Well, who did?' asked Tom.

'I don't know, but it certainly wasn't me! All I know is that when I returned to his apartment it was empty and he was gone. I did not kill him – I loved him,' Pearce kept repeating. He continued saying the same thing over and over as he was led back to his cell.

The two men left the prison and made their way back to Tom's home, pleased to find that the girls had prepared a nice barbecue in the garden. Soon they were munching on hotdogs and pizza, home-made by Cassie.

With the children put to bed, the grown-ups were sitting around in the glow of the numerous candles spread around the garden. Tom realised just how pretty his wife looked by candlelight, and secretly made plans to take advantage of her other talents not associated with cooking. It had been a trying time for everyone and it seemed that lovemaking had somehow slipped from the recently married couple's agenda.

The meeting with Pearce was brought up and the men

were relating what had been said, almost for their own benefit as much as for Cassie and Allison. It did not make sense and they sat quietly for a while, drinking their wine and deep in thought.

It was Cassie who ventured the first possible solution. 'Perhaps the Countess managed to get the paintings back?'

Tom looked blankly at his wife. 'How?'

'She could have used Pearce.'

It was Trevor's turn to ask, 'How?'

Allison, who had been relatively silent on all this until now, came in with, 'By using Hans to trick Pearce into revealing where the pictures were and he in turn informed the Countess of this.'

Trevor looked questioningly at his wife. 'How did she do that, do you think? So far as we know she had no connection with Hans.'

'So far as you know...' Allison sighed. 'Well, you're the "policeman", darling, go and find out.' She smiled, having enjoyed saying that. After all, she had been kept in the dark all these years about him being a policeman of sorts, so let him find out – she was not going to do his job for him.

They all laughed and the conversation turned to other everyday things until the girls retired to bed. The two men sat well into the night going over and over again the theories suggested by the two girls. Could they be right? Was the Countess right up to her slender neck in all this?

'Pearce could be partially correct in that Jonathan somehow managed to retain some of the pictures,' Tom ventured. 'The Countess would have been livid if that were true. A real falling out amongst thieves! And if you think about it, Allison's got a point. Bringing Hans into the equation makes sense – the missing link, if you like. He could have been working for the

Countess and passing on whatever he gleaned from Pearce. It might also explain why Pearce killed him – if he found out.'

'And why he then attempted to kill Jonathan. Maybe Trisha just got in the way?' Trevor mused. 'My lovely wife is right about one thing: we must go and find out!'

When the two men finally parted company and headed for bed, Tom found to his dismay that Cassie had already drifted deep into dreamland. 'Not tonight, Josephine,' he murmured to himself, looking wistfully at his gorgeous wife as he slid into bed beside her.

Chapter Thirty-Five

Following their long conversation, both Trevor and Tom had come to the conclusion that the first angle to check was the possible involvement of the mysterious Hans Geist. Had Pearce murdered him? Given his repeated protestations of love, it seemed unlikely, but if not then who? While Tom was certain that Pearce had carried out the shooting of Trish and Jonathan (Jonathan would have been rather silly to shoot himself after all!), he was not so sure about Hans. Trevor agreed and, according to the police surgeon's report, it was carried out at close range so was likely to have been someone Hans knew.

Trevor contacted the Italian police with whom he had worked before and asked for more information about Hans. They came back with a strange result. It seemed that the man, together with a woman identified as his sister, had started up a detective agency of all things just six months before. Within a short time, they were struggling to keep it afloat but, judging by their bank balance, things suddenly improved. They had received several thousand euros, which had been paid in cash into their account. Strangely, since Hans's death, the sister – name of Greta – had cleared out the account and disappeared. Photographs supplied by the Italian police showed that the woman was of a similar age to Cassie and Jessica. In addition to the sister going missing, so had the new Porsche that Hans had purchased just a month before. The Porsche had since been found abandoned in Paris.

*

Jonathan had managed to find himself a place to rent in the southern part of Italy near Sorrento, a place he knew well. He still needed to get his wound dressed on a regular basis and had found a local doctor willing to treat him. He knew he would have to sell one of the paintings shortly or he would run out of money. He managed to find a loan shark who was amenable to lending him some cash for a high interest payback. Jonathan knew he was on borrowed time; if he did not get rid of a painting he surely would find himself being fitted with some concrete boots, a prospect he was not at all keen on. But the risk was very high and Jonathan was living on a knife edge.

When Trevor related to Tom the findings of the Italian police, Tom was even more convinced that Hans Geist had somehow been involved with Connie Pasteur. He came up with an idea: he and Trevor should return to France and put Madame Connie under surveillance. He had a hunch that perhaps the woman known as Greta might just be with Connie at the château.

Trevor agreed. He knew their options were limited, to say the least, but finding the dead Hans's car abandoned in Paris was a lead, however slim. And so, having obtained permission from Paul to involve Tom and with tongue-in-cheek assurances given to Cassie that he would not in any circumstances be allowed near the Countess, the two men made their departure and headed back to France.

Because of its prominent position in the landscape, it would have been difficult to observe the château without being seen were it not for Trevor's know-how. With some of the high-powered surveillance equipment available to him, the two men were soon situated in the attic of a house close by, able to observe the occupants' daily goings-on – or would have been, had there been any. After two days of inactivity and stifling boredom, Tom was all for creating a diversion, but Trevor counselled patience.

On the third day, when Trevor was observing the château and Tom was idly leafing through a magazine, the Rolls at last emerged from the gates.

'Tom, you were right,' Trevor said gleefully, 'she is here. Remind me to get you a job with the department! Connie's in the back seat and I'm certain that's Greta Geist beside her. Have a look. They're heading for the village.'

'No, thanks,' Tom grinned, gazing down the telescopic lens, 'not enough money in it, and I've given up the sex part of the job!'

'Eh?' Trevor looked stupefied. 'What sex part? I reckon I've been missing out somewhere!'

Tom laughed. 'Don't worry, it is very much overrated.'

Trevor grinned. 'Seriously though, I guess we have gone as far as we can at present. Strictly speaking, neither woman is breaking any law so far as we know. We can't confront them without proof. We really need to find out what their next move will be – if any.'

'Yes, I agree.' Tom nodded. 'Connie has all that money from the five paintings we sold, and Greta has all Hans's money, so it's quite possible the two women mean to live the high life and enjoy it all together.'

Trevor had been thinking. 'You don't suppose...' His voice tailed away and he frowned.

'What?' Tom drew back from the lens and turned to look at his friend.

'Well, I was just wondering... I'm not sure why Connie

has this woman Greta trailing around with her – is there any possibility that the two might be having a sexual relationship?'

Tom burst out laughing and shook his head vigorously. 'I doubt it, Trevor. That woman is one hundred per cent whole woman!' He fell silent as he remembered the last kitchen table episode. Connie a lesbian? No, it wasn't possible. Madame Pasteur's appetite could never be satisfied by a woman.

Thinking that Tom was being a little naive, Trevor raised his eyebrows but said nothing. Instead he called the local police and arranged for them to keep track of the two women so that he and Tom could return to Italy to see what else they could do in finding Jonathan and the pictures. Trevor reasoned that if the recently wounded man was on his own, it would be almost impossible for him to travel about with all the paintings.

The police in Italy were carrying out spot checks on vans that might accommodate such a load, but had so far come up with nothing. It pointed to Jonathan having an accomplice.

Jonathan had made phone calls to several of his father's oldest contacts; people whom he knew would be interested in the two paintings with no questions asked. One of these was a man called Dudley Stewart, a fellow American who had lived in Italy for most of his life with the advantage that, unlike Jonathan, he spoke Italian fluently. Dudley was indeed a man of action. If he couldn't place the pictures, it was unlikely that anyone could.

Dudley had lost no time in travelling to Sorrento. He had looked at the two paintings and could not believe his eyes. Yes, they could well be originals, he said, and yes, he might well be able to move them – back in the USA. Jonathan was pleased; here was a fellow American who had all the contacts and, what was more, Jonathan could then return to the States and retire on the proceeds – well, at least live in some comfort. Florida appealed to him at that moment. The only problem was how to get the two paintings out of Italy and into the USA.

Trevor was sceptical about Tom's assurances that Madame Connie was all she appeared to be. Admittedly he had not been privileged to receive any of her personal attentions, but seeing the Greta woman turn up at the château made no sense to him. There had to be a something more to connect the two women.

He turned to his fellow Italian contacts and asked for further checks on Greta Geist. They did not take long to get back to him. Of course the woman's a lesbian, he was told; everyone knew that – didn't they mention it before? Sorry, they had not thought it was relevant. They then went on to add more information that somehow they had overlooked before.

Trevor replaced the phone on the hook and turned to Tom. 'I have it on the best authority that the Geist woman is a lesbian so, coupled with Hans being homosexual, the two made quite a pair – not that I'm prejudiced,' he added hastily. 'More to the point, Tom, the two were the offspring of a German father whose own father was in the SS. Given what you told me about Connie Pasteur, that surely must be too much of a coincidence?'

Tom's eyes widened and he nodded. Trevor's assumption that Madame Connie was up to her lovely neck in all this appeared to be correct. Even so, he still had a problem agreeing that his past lover could possibly, by any stretch of the imagination, be a lesbian!

Further checks uncovered that the Countess and her staff from the château had occupied a villa in the Tuscany area. The Countess had paid for four months' rent in advance, but she and her entourage had left suddenly before the four months were up and had not been heard of since. It would seem that they had left several belongings behind, almost as if they had departed in some haste. It was yet another factor to connect Madame Pasteur to the goings-on in Italy – if any more was needed.

Jonathan and his new accomplice had several things to do before they could attempt to ship the two paintings to the USA. First, Jonathan had to obtain a false American passport; not an easy task, but they could not take the chance of him being stopped at the airport or at the US Immigration. Since the recent terrorist attacks, things had become quite strict at the immigration centre in New York. Jonathan wanted desperately to get back to the US and recover some money on the stolen paintings. He considered he had earned it, having been shot like he had.

Before he and Tom left for Italy, Trevor decided to refine his observation of Madame Connie by arranging for a homing device to be placed on her car. It would save on manpower since it could be observed without having a man stationed permanently outside the château. From what he knew of her, Trevor was convinced that Connie would use the Rolls if she did go on an unscheduled long trip, so he had a French agent place the device on the chassis when the car was parked one day in the village. The Rolls could now be tracked by his French colleagues from the observation centre in the area. If and when she would make a move was anybody's guess, but it would be reported back to Trevor immediately.

In the château, things were not going smoothly. 'What does she want now?' cried an irate Daniel.

'Haven't a clue,' replied Anna. 'She's getting as bad as the Mistress. It was bad enough having Madame Connie throwing a tantrum, but this woman is nasty with it.'

Arthur Thomas, who was sitting in the kitchen having a cup of coffee, broke in, 'I agree. She thinks she owns the place and her screaming and shouting is getting on my nerves.'

'You're not the only one,' Daniel retorted. It seemed to them all that the German woman was now fully ensconced in the château and loving every minute of it.

Connie was content to let Greta take over the general running of the house and, as long as she performed her duties in the bedroom, Connie was happy. She often wondered to herself why her sexual preference had switched. She had never had any notion that she was in fact bisexual and the impromptu kiss those weeks ago had taken her by surprise, not to mention her response which had been so emphatic. If Tom Rendell could see her now, taking Greta to her bed with such vigour, he would be amazed to say the least, she thought. She was aware that AT was feeling left out, but that was his problem. Even she couldn't take on the two of them simultaneously!

For his part, Arthur Thomas couldn't decide if he felt insulted or relieved. That aside, he had used his role as the Countess's lover and pacifier to gain a little bit of power for himself. His regular sexual duties had been accepted by the other members of staff as essential to the wellbeing and harmony of the château. Now that his services were seemingly no longer required, he found he had lost the special esteem of the rest of the staff; he was just one of them. To make matters worse, he was getting nowhere with the lovely Susan. Despite getting her in many clinches that made her 'coo' and sweat, he had still not managed to score a home run. All this was making Arthur Thomas rather edgy, not to mention extremely frustrated. If this carried on, he thought sourly, he might even have to take himself in hand – something he had not done since he was fourteen. Heaven forbid!

Greta, now fully ensconced as Madame Connie's lover and companion, soon realised that Arthur Thomas was a threat to her. She had often caught Connie eyeing him up and it nettled her. Greta, of course, had no ambitions in that direction; she was an out and out lesbian of the kind that considered all males beneath her. She was so much more efficient and sexy than a mere man. Smiling to herself, Greta went over in her mind all her apparent attributes; she had more than enough to satisfy Connie Pasteur. Even so, she would keep an eye on Arthur Thomas.

The object of Greta's increasingly spiteful attention started thinking of ways to get rid of his nemesis; this person who had invaded all their lives and made his almost unbearable. Yes, she would have to go! Arthur Thomas knew that he and the rest of the staff would have to come up with a plan to get shot of this upstart woman. Lesbian indeed! He would show her. The German high priestess would get what was coming to her if he had anything to do with it.

Chapter Thirty-Six

At last the time had come for Jonathan and his friend to make their way to the United States with the pictures. Jonathan, with his newly acquired passport, would travel first. Dudley would follow on the next flight. He had arranged for the paintings to be taken into the airport cargo area the day before. A selected airport baggage handler would place one on the aircraft and another would remove it at the other end. It would then be carried through Customs without fear of them being stopped. They had agreed that Jonathan would take the first one – the Mona Lisa – and Dudley would travel with the Van Gogh. Jonathan had been assured that this procedure had been carried out several times before without a hitch.

Everything went like clockwork and Jonathan, after showing his boarding card, settled into his seat and ordered a large whisky. Great; things were going as planned and soon he would be sitting safely in his favourite bar in Manhattan drinking many more of these. He enjoyed the journey immensely; it was the first time in ages that he had managed to relax in such comfort and with the knowledge that he would soon receive five hundred thousand dollars for his share of the sale of the Mona Lisa. She would not be the only one with a smile on her face! Alighting from the plane, Jonathan made his way to the point where he had been told to collect the painting. He soon found his contact who identified himself by blowing his nose in a spotted red handkerchief. Without saying a word, the man left the trolley in front of Jonathan who promptly took hold of it.

He pushed it to the 'nothing to declare' exit only to be asked to wait while one of the staff examined his bag, hearing the dreaded words: 'What do you have here, Mr Fox?'

This was not supposed to happen! He had been told that he should just walk nonchalantly through the 'nothing to declare' area and all would be well. His heart sank as the Customs officer proceeded to open the case holding the painting. Jonathan took a deep breath; he would just declare that it was nothing more than a good copy, something he had picked up for a song in Rome.

'It certainly looks like a good copy,' the Customs officer was saying. Jonathan started feeling extremely queasy with the time being taken; after all he had been informed by Dudley that he would be ushered through by another paid helper. The man was speaking again, 'Can you confirm the title of the painting and who the artist might be?'

Jonathan stared at the officer in amazement. 'What do you mean? Don't you recognise a copy of the Mona Lisa when you see it?'

'Well, I would, sir. I do know the Mona Lisa, but this is certainly not she! More like a Van Gogh, I would say.'

'Don't be silly, it's a – ' Jonathan stopped short as he gazed upon the canvas. It was certainly not the Mona Lisa. His mind in a turmoil, he heard the Customs officer asking him to accompany him to a private room where he would be asked to explain how he had ended up with what looked remarkably like an original Van Gogh, and what he had been saying about the Mona Lisa? Either way, he was obviously not telling the truth. If he was implying that his declaration was wrong, it required a more thorough investigation.

Cursing to himself as he realised his new found 'friend'

had double-crossed him, Jonathan followed the officer to the interview room. There was certainly no honour amongst thieves, he thought bitterly.

Back in Italy, dragging on his large Cuban cigar and sipping his cognac, Dudley Stevens sat back in his chair. Not bad, he thought, looking at the smiling face of the Mona Lisa. He would now make contact with his fellow dealer and lifetime friend, Louis, who had assured him that the painting would fetch the two of them over thirty million euros each. It appeared that in certain circumstances the Vatican would always make an exception. Not bad for a day's work!

Arthur Thomas had noticed that Anna seemed to be the one on the receiving end of Greta's abuse and he soon realised that the most likely reason was because Anna was of Jewish origin. It appeared that Greta, being descended from a family with strongly held anti-Semitic views, could not help herself and was taking out her venom on the unfortunate girl. Greta's expression said it all: Anna was not fit to be working at the château and, what was more, she should not, in any way, be serving the mighty Greta Geist. Arthur Thomas was fairly sure that the German woman was poisoning her lesbian lover's mind about how badly Anna was performing: insolent, useless at doing her chores and so on. If only he could get close to Madame Connie, he might be able to undo some of the damage, but these days he was never alone with her. Arthur knew he must come up with a plan. He confided in Daniel who had great affection for Anna and was only too pleased to hear about a possible way of getting rid of the unwanted German priestess.

    Arthur Thomas was right: Greta was attempting to poison

Connie's mind against her servant. The problem was, however, that Connie had great affection for Anna, having received excellent service from her for many years. She had observed that Anna was becoming extremely distressed and that Daniel was going about like a bear with a sore head, and knew she ought to do something about it.

The crowning moment came when Greta was presented with a new Mercedes sports car. Connie had come up with the idea that if Greta had a nice car to drive around in she would ease off on Anna. Greta's obvious delight only inflamed the situation as far as Arthur Thomas and the rest of the staff were concerned. The satisfied smirk on Greta's face as she threw the keys to Arthur Thomas and told him to clean the car after only one trip was enough to make his blood boil. The woman had crossed the line and now she would get her comeuppance.

It was relatively easy to arrange. Madame Connie's collection of jewellery had always been left lying around. She trusted her staff implicitly; there had been no need for any safe or even locked doors. The diamonds that littered her dressing table were always there, gleaming brightly in the side-lighting that adorned the walls of her elaborate dressing room. Connie had even given Greta some of her smaller pieces, but she preferred to keep the larger items for herself – after all, as she often remarked, diamonds are a girl's best friend.

It was the chambermaid, Stella, who was chosen to plant the seed in Madame Connie's mind. There was no point in it being Anna since she might be accused of trying to get her own back on Greta, aside from which Stella had always taken personal care of the Countess's jewellery and furs so she was the perfect one to express her concerns when a small diamond bracelet went missing.

'It must be there somewhere,' the Countess remarked.

'Have a good look for it, Stella.' The search was fruitless; it was nowhere to be found. The Countess just shrugged and said nonchalantly, 'Oh well, it'll turn up.' Connie was not surprised when, later, spiteful innuendos were made by Greta against the servant Anna: she was after all a Jew and they loved all kinds of things such as diamonds, didn't they.

Connie smarted upon hearing this; she had no reason to suspect any of her staff and, even held in thrall to Greta as she was, found her lover's remarks unacceptable and refused to believe that Anna would ever steal from her.

The next item that went missing was even larger than the first, and this time Connie was more concerned; it was one of her favourite pieces. The following week was hectic – everywhere was searched and searched again. Nowhere was missed, not even the staff quarters. Greta had insisted that they search her room as well although, as she hated the idea of Anna touching her things, she allowed Daniel to carry out the search – but again nothing. A bad atmosphere ensued and they all went about with their faces glum and distrustful, each person imagining that the other was to blame – except those in the know. Daniel reported to Connie that morale at the château had never been so bad and if her 'guest' did not stop stirring it all up, Madame would soon lose most of her staff.

Connie could not understand how all this could be happening, but her suspicions fell on Arthur Thomas and she called him in and questioned him about his possible involvement. After all, she thought, he might have an axe to grind seeing that she had stopped her favours to him. His reaction was one of immense anger and Connie, convinced by his indignant denials, realised that any further insinuations would result in his leaving and possibly taking other staff with him. Looking at her chauffeur's tanned body revealed by his unbuttoned shirt, Connie experienced a jolt of desire and wanted suddenly to feel a man's naked skin against her own; a feeling she had almost forgotten about.

Recognising that lustful look, Arthur Thomas hesitated. He took a step towards her but she quickly looked away and told him to leave.

The last straw came when the largest and most expensive necklace went missing despite Connie's efforts to place all her jewellery under lock and key. 'That is it! I am calling in the police,' she cried.

The police soon arrived and, it being Madame Connie, they interviewed thoroughly all the staff and then searched the château. Nowhere was spared, not even Madame Connie's own room; after all, it could all be part of a gigantic insurance fraud. Finding nothing, they next turned their attention to the grounds.

The sergeant finally came in and asked to speak with the Countess privately. He had a stern look on his face. 'To whom does the Mercedes Sports belong?' he asked politely.

'My friend... Greta,' Connie replied. 'Why do you ask?'

Ignoring her question, the sergeant nodded. 'And how long has your friend been staying with you, Countess?'

Connie looked blankly at the sergeant. 'Getting on for a year now... but surely you don't suspect her?'

The sergeant reached into a bag he was holding and took out the missing diamonds. 'It would seem that they had all been stashed in a special compartment in the Mercedes and I would venture to suggest they have been there for some time.'

The staff of the château formed a line outside as the scowling and screaming Greta was led away. 'Bye, bye,' they mouthed as she was pushed unceremoniously into the waiting police car.

The atmosphere in the château changed immediately and

the staff settled back down to some normality in their lives. It was soon taken one step further when Arthur Thomas received a familiar demand to come to the Countess's bedroom. Madame Connie, it would seem, had quickly recovered from the shock of her lover's perfidy. Yes, life was sweet again and AT was now very much in the driving seat, in more ways than one!

Tom and Cassie were staying in their Italian home and getting used to having a child running around and getting into everything, as all children do once they learn to walk. Trevor's phone call informing him of Jonathan's arrest in New York came as a surprise to Tom, for while Jonathan was on the list of people to apprehend in both Europe and the US, it did seem strange for the notification to come through so quickly. Paul explained this, however: he had made enquiries following the receipt of an anonymous call made from a pay phone, the caller informing him that Jonathan Green was to get his comeuppance in New York. The chickens were certainly coming home to roost! Dudley smirked as he replaced the receiver – just another small end that needed tidying up!

A couple of weeks after Greta's arrest, Daniel and Anna were surprised to find their mistress walking around with a frown on her face; something had obviously happened to make her extremely cross. It did not take long for Daniel, the father figure of the staff, to find out that all charges against Greta had been dropped. This had occurred, evidently, after a personal phone call from Greta's solicitor to Madame Connie herself. Daniel came away with the impression that Greta had made Connie an offer she couldn't refuse. He and the rest of the staff were startled even further when someone arrived and collected the

Mercedes Sports; after all it was in Greta's name and with no charges she had obviously demanded, 'Car please!' The staff, most of whom knew exactly how the missing diamonds had got into the woman's car, waited for the axe to fall, afraid that Connie had found out about their scheme. They were both surprised and relieved when nothing more was said on the matter.

Connie, to whom it would never have occurred that her staff could be so underhand, had not had a choice. Veiled threats came via Greta's solicitor who, innocent of their true meaning, had advised Connie to back down. Knowing she was an accessory to murder, even though she had not been present when Greta had shot Hans, Connie agreed. Just knowing about it would be enough to make things seriously difficult for her.

Chapter Thirty-Seven

Dudley, fresh from his betrayal of Jonathan, had arrived at the meeting place he had arranged with Louis: a café which had been used several times over the past few months by different people all seemingly wanting to dispose of their paintings. In a way it had become Louis's outside office and, with Rome's morning sun shining brightly, Louis felt suddenly uplifted; now at last he would be the one receiving a good return for his connections. The Vatican, which normally paid him his commission, was as strict with his return as they were with their prices for the paintings they purchased. Theirs had always been a take-it-or-leave-it attitude. Louis had made up his mind; he had his own pension to think of. It would seem there was a price to fit everyone in certain circumstances.

Passing through St Peter's Square that day, Jessica, who was enjoying a brief holiday with Cassie and Tom, happened to see Louis talking to a man in the café – quite a handsome man as far as she could see. She decided to take the bull by the horns and introduce herself. She was dressed in an outfit that showed all her assets to the full and felt confident about her appearance.

Louis was not too keen on seeing her at that moment as he was about to confirm arrangements for the meeting at the Vatican in three days' time.

Dudley, for his part, was extremely pleased to meet this delightful lady from Paris who oozed sex and, to Louis's displeasure, invited her to join them.

It was obvious to Jessica that the two men were talking about art and knowing that art normally meant money she wondered if this American might just be an art dealer. Surprise, surprise, he was, and that could only mean one thing – hard cash. Jessica's talents for collecting information had not dwindled over the last few months and she managed to find out the address of the apartment block where Dudley was residing. Even discovering that he had a long-term girlfriend in the US didn't put her off and she squeezed Dudley's hand as she made her farewell. The look that Dudley gave her as she did this could mean only one thing: yes, I'm interested. Dudley's loaded invitation for Jessica to drop by soon did not fall on deaf ears.

Returning to Tom and Cassie's, Jessica had an excuse ready for missing out on the evening's entertainment of television followed by more television! All she would convey to Cassie was that she was meeting a friend of the art dealer Louis, a man called Dudley – and he was extremely good-looking.

Cassie wished her well but, remembering Gregorio aka Pearce and knowing Jessica's penchant for picking up unsuitable men, she added a note of caution to her farewell hug. 'Call us if you're going to be late getting back,' she said with a smile. She knew only too well that if Jessica was on the way to scoring a new notch on her bedpost she could sometimes lose track of time – and why not indeed?

Greta was now free to do what she wanted. Charges against her had been dropped. She was fully aware that she had been set up by the staff of the château. That part of her revenge could wait; she now had to get her hands on some cash. The money given to her by the Countess was still in her bank account.

In the past, Greta had always been of the opinion that she was better at playing the detective than her deceased brother, Hans. She now had the chance to prove it. It was made a lot easier for her when she read in the newspaper that the man in question had been arrested in New York and would be returned to Italy to stand trial on smuggling charges. Good; that was one down then.

Without proof, the authorities in New York had been unable to bring a charge of smuggling against Jonathan. That would have to be proved later if and when the Countess could be persuaded to press charges, she being the legal owner at the time. It would be left to Trevor and Paul to do the persuading, for once without Tom, since Cassie even now would not countenance a further trip by her vulnerable husband into the lair of Madame Connie. It was a definite no-go as far as Cassie was concerned. 'You can't be serious!' she had told Trevor when he had called to suggest yet another excursion to the château.

Jessica set off for the apartment which she understood was owned by Dudley, art dealer and man of distinction. The latter description was purely Jessica's fantasy; she wanted to find out just how distinctive his bank balance could be. She was the only one in the original set-up – excluding poor Trish, of course – who was not earning big bucks. Cassie and Tom were now settled in every way, both financially and sexually, and while Jessica still had her job in Paris, she had come to the conclusion that eventually her position there could change if the recession continued.

Finding the apartment number proved easy; she simply looked at the postal boxes in the hallway of the smart apartment block: number 101. Jessica had already stopped off at the wine merchants and purchased a good bottle of red wine, just in case!

It was eight in the evening as she tapped on the door, hoping Dudley would be in. Her tap was met by silence; that was until she heard the door bolts being withdrawn. Dudley was there in his robe, having obviously showered and shaved as if he was expecting a visitor – could that visitor be her?

'Come in, Jessica. I was hoping you might call.' He gave her a warm smile.

The scene was set and Jessica knew that all her latent instincts had been proven correct – the man appeared ready for action and, if that's what the man wanted, she was just the one to make sure he got it!

Greta was making progress. She had carried out her own research into her past connections with her grandfather in the Third Reich. She soon found out that, like Connie, she was able to identify relatives she had not known existed. She was pleased to learn that she had several cousins living in France and Italy. It would be relatively easy to look them up and might prove beneficial. Either way she had nothing to lose and everything to gain.

The man answering the door was obviously of German stock. He had fair hair and was sturdily built; rather pug-nosed, but clean shaven. Upon being invited in, Greta was amazed at the paraphernalia that adorned the walls of the small villa which was situated just outside Rome. It was like walking into the past: large German flags sporting swastikas; and portraits of Hitler and many of his henchmen hung on the walls. Looking around, it made Greta, Germanic as she was, shudder as she viewed the scene. She had done her homework well. In addition to being a close cousin, Otto was an ex-military man who had been discharged from the present German army due to his extreme fascist views. In modern Germany such views were no longer tolerated; well at least, not in public.

Otto offered Greta a drink of schnapps which she accepted although she did feel it was a little early to start drinking. Her new found cousin did not seem to share her concern and poured himself another large measure. It was not hard to make friends with Otto; he was getting more amenable as the minutes passed. Yes, he knew plenty of contacts in the art world, and yes, anyone selling paintings that belonged to the cause would be tracked down and dealt with. Greta was getting a much more aggressive response than she had bargained for. Otto's only thoughts at that moment were to further his underground party's cause. Greta finally managed to discover that there were around thirty such party activists in the area and most of them came to Otto's villa for regular monthly meetings. It happened that tonight such a meeting was taking place and, after subjecting Greta to a number of searching questions about her views, Otto invited her to attend.

Chapter Thirty-Eight

The bottle of red wine was only half empty when Jessica pulled her new friend into his bedroom. There was not much resistance as she pushed Dudley back onto his bed and pulled apart his robe to reveal his olive-skinned body, the sight of which pleased her greatly. Briefly remembering the incident with 'Gregorio', Jessica knew that at least this time she would not be forgetting anything that was about to happen. Not a pack of pretzels in sight; what on earth had happened to all the normal accepted procedures of wining and dining before the event? Jessica smiled to herself; she fully intended to make a meal of everything. Weeks of enforced celibacy needed satisfying and she soon found that the man now sharing the bed had what she required: a lot of energy and stamina. Time and again she made him rise to the occasion and time and again she had to lie back to catch her breath. Dudley was a cool character and his idea of lovemaking was simple: the woman should do most of the work and he would just attempt to wear her out. Fair enough; that suited Jessica.

It seemed that the effort put in by both parties had the desired effect. It was late in the evening when the two lovers rushed to catch a meal in one of the late-night eateries. Jessica was extremely happy to pay for this on her company credit card. If Tom Rendell thought he was off the hook, he had another thought coming; hit them in the pocket still ruled when scorned women took their revenge. As far as Jessica was concerned, Tom had not finished paying yet.

*

The group of Third Reich supporters grew until the lounge was full, forcing some of the party to spill out into the garden. Wine and schnapps flowed freely and Greta found herself enjoying the banter that went with the occasion. She was even more taken with events when she met another woman in the group, a Nazi but with yearnings, it seemed, for company of the same sex. The two women eyed each other up as they waltzed around the preliminaries of a meeting that they both knew would end with sexual pleasure. Mata was a very forceful person; she had an air of superiority which, in Greta's view, could only come from someone of good German stock. Mata was the obvious equal of all the men attending the meeting that evening and all the men, including Otto, treated her with great respect. Was it possible, Greta wondered, that the next leader of the Third Reich, Mach Two, could possibly be a woman?

The possibility of Greta and Mata meeting up later that evening was crushed when Mata confirmed that she had a further meeting to go to in the next city; one she had to attend if they were going to move forward with increasing their following. Greta nodded her understanding and accepted the note that Mata secreted into her hand. Even in the modern German order, same sex relationships were still frowned upon by some people. If the two had any future together they would have to tread carefully when arranging their trysts.

As the last of their group bade their farewells, Otto, already well oiled from the evening's drinking, asked Greta to stay behind in order that he could show her a list of contacts which he considered they should start with first thing in the morning. It would not take long, he urged. Greta agreed. Walking to the room upstairs seemed innocent enough, but when Otto closed and locked the door Greta knew instantly that this man had more than names on his mind. The room was dark and gloomy; by a small light in the corner she could see an unmade bed, just as someone had left it that morning.

She was not having it and pushed Otto away as he sought to push her towards the bed. 'You must be joking,' she said, looking at him in total disbelief.

Otto smiled, reaching for her. 'Playing hard to get, eh? Come on, you've been begging for it all day!'

Greta was now screaming and punching him on his chest; eventually she managed to knee him in the groin. What followed was not at all pretty. Otto's smile changed to a snarl and he smashed Greta across the face with such force that she fell back stunned and bleeding onto the bed. She knew there was little she could do to avoid what was coming and felt sick with loathing for this brutish man, her skin crawling with repulsion.

Tearing away at her blouse and then at her skirt, both of which came off with ease such was the force he used, Otto, now at the height of his arousal, sweated and panted above her. His eyes were crazed revealing that he was beyond reason. Ignoring her tearful pleading, he ripped the remaining garments from her legs. As far as Otto was concerned she just happened to be a woman in the right place at the right time. He was intent on satisfying his pent-up needs and there was nothing Greta could do about it.

Dudley was feeling totally relaxed: first he had managed to obtain a painting that would give him wealth he had previously only dreamt of, and now he had been bedded by this wildcat who had picked him up from the café. Sometimes God moves in mysterious ways, he thought, pondering his good fortune. He resolved to spend the next twenty-four hours putting a smile on Jessica's delightful face and keeping it there.

Jessica was also extremely relaxed. She sent a brief text message to Cassie to say she was fine, having a good time and unlikely to be back that night. Jessica added a smiley at the end of her text; she would not be availing herself of her comfy bed at Cassie's – not when she was warming someone else's.

Silently weeping, Greta raised herself from the crumpled bed and staggered to the bathroom where she was violently sick. Looking in the mirror, she was horrified to see her face was black and blue and one eye half closed. There were bruises on her arms and legs – all over her body, in fact. Her evil cousin had not spared her in any way. Greta had no time to look for a means of escape; a hand grabbed her neck and she felt herself being dragged back into the darkened bedroom and thrown again onto the bed. It seemed Otto was not finished with her yet and Greta, keeping herself sane by imagining all the ways in which she might eventually exact her revenge, resigned herself to the inevitable.

The following morning, Dudley was in such a good mood that he started to boast to Jessica about being a successful businessman as well as a great lover. It all came out about him having a fantastic painting to sell which, according to his friend Louis, was going to make him into a millionaire in the next day or so.

He was so full of himself that Jessica started to take notice of what he was actually saying, but when she asked what this fantastic painting was, he simply smiled at her and tapped a finger to his nose which made her all the more curious. Having been brought up to date by Tom and Cassie about the search for Madame Connie's stolen collection, Jonathan's arrest and the recovery of the Van Gogh, it occurred to Jessica that Dudley might not be everything he seemed and she determined to find out more.

She made her excuses to him so that she could leave and get a change of clothes, but she genuinely wanted to meet him again that evening. Aside from the fact that the sex had been great, she knew instinctively that something was going on here. She meant to keep track of her lover and the painting he refused to name.

Arriving back at Tom and Cassie's villa, she quickly sought out Tom who was very interested in what she had to say. Tom immediately phoned Trevor who confirmed that he and Paul would catch the next plane out to Italy. This was too a good a chance to miss, and it did sound promising. In the meantime, Paul was having Dudley's background checked out by their contacts in Italy.

By the time Paul and Trevor got off the plane at Leonardo da Vinci Airport, they knew all about Dudley and his association with Jonathan. They wondered about his association with Louis whom they had always considered to be an honest dealer. Now they had begun to have some doubts.

With this information, Paul had a dilemma: his standing instruction from the European Government was that he kept Madame Connie up to date with all developments concerning her paintings. Tom had recently returned to the Countess (via a third party) the two smaller paintings that he had purchased with Louis. There was no way Cassie would have been allowed to return them to the Countess in person.

Ignoring Trevor's pleas to keep her out of it for now, at least until they were sure Dudley had one of her paintings in his possession and, if so, to recover it themselves, he called Madame Connie.

Connie was feeling sorry for herself; she was in bed with an extremely bad cold when the call came. Having been assured by Paul that it might just be a 'possible' recovery but they were not yet certain it was one of hers, Connie almost let slip that if it was, it could only be the Mona Lisa, since the missing Van Gogh had already been recovered from Jonathan. However, she never let on that she had all but two of her paintings safely back in her hidden room. Connie's biggest fear was that the authorities would take them all away from her if they investigated the paintings' origin and discovered they were not rightfully hers. She continued to hope that somehow she would be able to keep them in secret and so she said nothing to Paul, beyond the fact that she would send her man Arthur Thomas to be there to collect the painting if it was indeed recovered. Where should he meet them?

Ending the call, Connie blew her nose and moaned. If there was even a chance of retrieving the Mona Lisa, she wanted it back with minimum delay even though she might eventually lose it to the authorities. With this cold however, the last thing she fancied was a trip to Italy that could turn out to be fruitless. No, Arthur Thomas would have to go – and he could travel by train.

Arthur Thomas was not too upset about going to sunny Rome; he had been out the night before on a useless attempt to separate Susan from her father which had ended as usual in tears. He now accepted that it was just about a lost cause, but he was not too concerned; after all, he still had his château duties to carry out!

Dudley was cock-a-hoop; he had arranged to meet Jessica that evening at the local restaurant and was fondly anticipating things to come: the way this lady took control and dominated him in bed. Just thinking about how Jessica had repeatedly taken advantage of his aroused passions gave him an erection that refused to lie down. Yes, there certainly was an art to lovemaking and he could be proud of how he had accommodated the lady in question.

Trevor suggested that Jessica carried on as if nothing had changed. She should meet Dudley at the restaurant in order that everyone could get a good look at him. The bird was being made ready to be plucked, gutted and quartered. Whatever Jessica chose to do that evening after the meal was entirely up to her.

Arthur Thomas alighted from the train and made his way to the hotel that had been designated as his overnight stay; just the one night, it was not meant to be a holiday, Connie had said. Trevor and Paul would contact him there early in the evening and then the three of them would make their way to the restaurant. Tom and Cassie would join them there, and they would all sit down to a slap-up dinner. You can't beat mixing a little business with pleasure, Arthur thought happily.

It was the first time Arthur Thomas had been in company of English people since the dramatic rescue of his lady boss and the rest of her staff from certain death, and he was starting to enjoy himself. He now knew everything about the estate agent and his wanton use of Madame Connie, but he had taken an instant liking to Tom and, of course, his delightful wife; she was something else. Cassie reminded him very much of Susan; perhaps they were related? He put this silly thought behind him as he refilled everyone's glass.

The cost of the dinner would be on Madame Connie who had graciously given AT her credit card as if to remind everyone that she was still around. This 'generosity' did not go amiss with Tom and Cassie!

Halfway through the evening, Jessica and Cassie met up by chance in the ladies' powder room and walked back into the dining area together, still talking earnestly. Trevor groaned; he could see Dudley looking at the two girls as they made their way back to their respective tables. Didn't Jessica realise she risked blowing their cover?

Noticing Cassie was not hard to do and Dudley, always inquisitive, asked the question: 'Who is she and who's that she's with?' Jessica was momentarily stuck for words, but she remarked that Cassie used to work at the same office as she many years before and it was a happy coincidence to see her again after all this time. She didn't know who she was with – why?

This seemed to satisfy Dudley but did not prevent him sending over a bottle of champagne. It seemed the would-be millionaire was already splashing the cash!

'Cheers,' they chorused, lifting their glasses of champers in Dudley's direction.

'See you in court,' Paul mouthed silently as he sipped at the contents.

Chapter Thirty-Nine

It was comparatively easy for Greta to leave the bedroom where she had just experienced the worst night of her life. Her attacker was snoring loudly in apparent contentment as she dressed and hurriedly left the house, her eyes blackened and red from crying; her body aching from the abuse she had suffered by the evil man. She would make him pay, but how? The chances were that the police would not take any action as she had apparently stayed back after the party and had gone willingly up to his bedroom. Greta made her way to where she knew she might just get some sympathy; she went directly to Mata's address. Knocking on the door she was met by Mata who straightaway knew that something really bad had happened to her. It did not take long for the sorry tale to be related and Mata just stood there in disbelief. She knew Otto was a pig but how could he have gone so far as to rape his own cousin, for God's sake – and what is more, she was a lesbian. Whether Otto had realised it or not, as far as Mata was concerned that made his crime even worse.

Mata told Greta to take a shower and get herself some food. She had to go out for a while but she would return and they would talk again. Greta, still in shock, scrubbed herself down with hot soapy water. Afterwards, she managed to make herself some coffee but could not even think about food. She had hoped for more kind words from Mata but her new friend had not yet returned. All Greta wanted was to cleanse herself.

Showering again and again did not even begin to make her feel clean. As she calmed down a little, she started to think about revenge and cursed herself for not taking one of the Lugers she had seen displayed on a shelf beneath that rat Otto's gross display of German flags and other regalia. It would be easy enough to shoot a pig like Otto; a lot easier than shooting her own brother – and that had not been particularly difficult. The swine had ruined her life and Greta knew she had to get even, regardless of the consequences.

Jessica spent another active night in Dudley's apartment and once more enjoyed herself – and him – to the full. By the time the next day dawned, she knew exactly what he had in his possession, what he was going to do with it, and where he was going and when. It was simple to pass this information on to the others. Jessica felt a slight pang of regret for Dudley was an excellent lover. On the other hand, he had been in cahoots with that rat Jonathan and she wanted nothing more to do with him. She waited until she could hear him singing in the shower then made a quick call on her mobile.

Dudley, still singing, came grinning out of the bathroom and proceeded to make himself sufficiently presentable to receive – what was it? Thirty million euros? He could just about get used to that!

At the appointed hour, Louis arrived at the café, the designated meeting place, in order that he and Dudley could both go with the painting to the Vatican at the pre-arranged time of twelve noon. Sitting there in the sunshine, he apparently had no idea that he would soon have further company. First it was Tom who sat down at the same table as if it were a chance meeting and proceeded to engage him in small talk. Moments later, they were joined by Trevor and Paul. The late arrival of Dudley, red in the face and carrying a parcel, caused an extremely embarrassing few minutes that left both Louis and Dudley glancing at their watches, anxious not to miss their noon appointment. (After all, sixty million euros waits for no one!) When the uncomfortable party was joined by a clean-shaven, spruced-up Arthur Thomas, it suddenly became clear to Dudley that all was not what it seemed. He glanced quickly around the café, looked hesitantly at Louis, grabbed his parcel and half rose from his chair.

He was way too late. Paul had been merely biding his time until everyone was in place. He beckoned over the two plainclothes police officers who had arrived some time before and were sitting nearby drinking coffee, awaiting the signal to detain the unfortunate Dudley.

Dropping all pretence that this was a chance meeting, Trevor frowned at Louis and asked, 'Does the Vatican still wish to go ahead with the purchase of the painting?' Louis nodded meekly which they took as the affirmative.

Dudley just could not believe it as he was led away by the policemen. His face crumpled, angry tears springing to his eyes as he saw Trevor and Louis walking off towards the Vatican with Arthur Thomas, carrying his precious painting and apparently going to collect what was to have been his future. He covered his face with his hands and wept for his thirty million euros.

'What goes around comes around,' Tom murmured, watching the pathetic American being bundled into the police car that had just drawn up at the kerb.

'I doubt you're talking about London buses,' Paul quipped with a grin as they hurried to catch up with Trevor, Louis and Arthur Thomas.

Louis had been feeling mightily relieved since Arthur Thomas had remarked that Connie Pasteur had given him the authority to sell the Mona Lisa. A bird in the hand is worth two in the bush, thought Louis. He had been having visions of receiving nothing at all out of the deal as soon as it was known the painting had been recovered. He knew if he messed around in any way with the Vatican he would jeopardise his excellent connections, but as it was he would at least get some commission, if not as much as he had envisaged. By keeping his options open and cooperating with Paul and Trevor, he appeared to have got away with his questionable dealings with Jonathan and Dudley.

Their arrival at the Vatican was similar to the last time Louis and Tom had attended a meeting with His Eminence but this time, due to Arthur Thomas being there to represent Madame Connie, a request was made for Trevor and Paul to remain outside the meeting room. It would seem that His Eminence did not like too many witnesses to the proceedings which, as usual, were not up for discussion.

Paul and Trevor sat talking in the hall, taking in the splendour that surrounded them. It was like being in another world. Paul twiddled with his cufflinks that glittered in the subdued lighting of the hallway and caught Trevor's attention. He remembered his conversation with Tom who of course had received a similar set from Connie. 'They're very nice, Paul. Where did you get them?' he asked, hiding a smile.

Paul was startled and his face flushed; it was a straightforward question but what could he say? His sixth sense told him that Trevor's question was loaded; perhaps he knew more than he was letting on. His thoughts went back to the time when Tom had leaned forward and said 'Snap!' Great, Paul thought, his cover must have been blown. He looked

Trevor straight in the eye and, calling his bluff, remarked, 'Madame Connie gave them to me.'

Trevor stared back, but could only mutter, 'You lucky bugger!'

Greta had showered yet again; she felt so unclean, she was bruised all over and ached both in her mind and body. She was still trying desperately to come to terms with what had taken place. Sitting in Mata's lounge, she would have liked a little more sympathy and understanding from her new friend but she knew Mata was made of sterner stuff than she and would most likely have taken rape in her stride.

Mata poured herself a cup of coffee and looked at Greta's swollen face. 'I think you had better stay here for a few days, Greta, to recover from your ordeal. Then we can make plans for the future. Yes?'

'Thank you.' Greta nodded her agreement. She did not fancy going back to her own house. 'I would love to.'

In the Vatican, His Eminence's usual three experts were looking closely at the painting of the Mona Lisa. The three men seemed to take an age and kept moving the painting around to get a better look at it. They finally stood, nodding to each other and then in turn towards His Eminence who got up, walked to the window and looked out. Without turning, he spoke.

'We have a serious problem with the provenance of all the paintings we have purchased from Madame Pasteur. The paintings are indeed excellent and, so far as we are able to ascertain, they are as genuine as the others that hang in Rome, Paris and here in the Vatican. The value of most of these paintings is beyond price and the monies we have advanced to you only reflect a part of their value.'

He turned from the window at last and looked across at Louis. 'As far as this particular painting is concerned, however, we have to withhold part of the sixty million euros we offered for it when you first approached us, Louis. I am sure that in the circumstances you will not be surprised. We will retain thirty million and release to Arthur Thomas the remaining thirty million. Once our experts, who will include many others not associated with us, have looked again at the painting and are happy with its authenticity, we will release the balance.'

Tom shrugged his shoulders and looked enquiringly at Arthur Thomas. He was Madame Connie's representative and it was up to him. Arthur Thomas seemed to take it in his stride; he just remarked that would be fine and handed over the bank account details. Louis looked down at the floor and said nothing.

The group shook hands and made their way from the Holy City, collecting Paul and Trevor on the way. Arthur Thomas, who had shown remarkable business acumen throughout and was clearly enjoying his important role, informed the group that they would have to wait until the money had been received in Madame Connie's bank account before Tom and Louis could receive their finder's fee.

As far as Trevor and Paul were concerned, of course, since they worked for the British Government their share would be nil. However, Arthur Thomas said, he would suggest to Madame Connie that she make a substantial donation to a charity of their choice.

Paul immediately agreed to this, looking enquiringly at Trevor, and said, 'That's a splendid idea. May I suggest "Save the Children"?'

Trevor nodded. 'Excellent choice,' he murmured.

That agreed, Arthur Thomas made his excuses, explaining that he had to return to the château and report back to Madame Connie. He could not stay and enjoy their company, but he was sure they would understand. The others nodded and, thanking him, shook him by the hand and wished him well.

Tom was pleased that the part he had played in recovering the Mona Lisa and apprehending Dudley had been recognised, but he refused the finder's fee, agreeing that any money due to him should also be paid to a charity of his choice. Cassie would have to wait for her new curtains. He smiled as he imagined her face when he told her the news. She wouldn't really mind; he knew his wife was just happy having him around, not to mention their son Peter.

Louis found himself unable to share in everyone's high spirits. He would now have to wait a long time to get his usual commission from the Vatican, and he could hardly explain he had been hoping to split the sixty million with Dudley! He sighed to himself; his efforts at intrigue had all turned pear-shaped. He wasn't really cut out for it, he decided. He might just as well go back to being legit – it paid better!

Jonathan had been returned to Italy and was now in jail facing a lengthy custodial sentence. Each day that passed, he promised himself that if he ever got out of that wretched place and got his hands on Dudley, all hell would break loose. So it was with utter amazement that he woke one morning to find his old friend sitting glumly in the next cell.

Rubbing his eyes in disbelief, Jonathan rolled off his bunk and walked the short distance to the bars that separated their two cells. Peering through, he suddenly jabbed a finger at the squirming Dudley and exploded, 'It's you! Come here, you bastard. I want a word with you.'

Dudley attempted a smile and between gritted teeth managed to ease out the words, 'Hullo Jonathan, er… how are you?' He felt sick to his stomach. His day was turning out even more badly than he had figured. What was worse, he knew that unavoidably some time, somewhere, sooner or later, he was in for the beating of his life. It had not taken Jonathan long to work out who had made certain phone calls to the American authorities.

Greta was watching television. She knew enough Italian to understand the news reports but what she saw surprised her: police were seen leaving a house that she thought she recognised. They were carrying out someone on a stretcher; clearly a dead body since it was encased in a black plastic bag. Suddenly, she placed the house and at the same time the familiar face of Otto flashed up on the screen. It would seem that someone had entered his villa and shot him directly between the eyes with one of his own Luger pistols. Greta swung round as she heard Mata enter the room behind her. 'Hey, Mata, guess what's happened! Otto's been…' Her voice tailed away as she saw her friend glance at the television and shrug.

'Really? How very unfortunate,' Mata said nonchalantly.

Greta got up from her chair and walked unsteadily across the room to take her lover in her arms, managing, despite her bruised mouth, to plant a big kiss on Mata's lips. 'Now that's what I call a friend,' she murmured huskily.

A week after their meeting at the Vatican, Paul received a surprise phone call from Madame Connie who wanted to know how things had gone. Paul, always cautious about giving away any information, said, 'I'm sorry, but why you are asking me that, Madame Pasteur?'

Madame Connie was seemingly not amused. 'What do you mean? It's surely not an unreasonable question,' she shouted angrily down the phone. 'What happened at the meeting – are the negotiations still going on? Where's Arthur Thomas? I've heard nothing from him. I had expected him back by now.'

'Is he not with you, Madame Connie?' Paul asked politely, placing the call on loudspeaker and beckoning to Trevor who had just come in.

'No, he is not and what's more, neither is my Mona Lisa!'

'Forgive me for asking but, if you haven't heard from Arthur Thomas, how can you possibly know it was that particular painting we recovered?' Paul asked, winking at Trevor.

There was a silence on the other end of the phone.

'Well,' Paul continued when it was apparent that the Countess was momentarily stumped for words, 'all I can tell you, Madame Pasteur, is that Arthur Thomas left us with a certified cashier's cheque for thirty million euros. Are you saying you haven't got that either?' Paul knew very well that the money would have been paid into a bank account which clearly had not been Madame Connie's, but he wanted to get his own back for a certain DVD!

Paul turned down the speaker in an attempt to extinguish the tirade of abuse that came from the lady at the other end. Lady? No lady would surely have any knowledge of words like that! After a moment he replaced the receiver, cutting off Madame Connie in mid-sentence.

Trevor laughed. 'It would seem that Arthur Thomas has been well paid for his services – a lot more than a set of diamond cufflinks – wouldn't you say, Paul?'

Paul grinned and nodded. 'Touché, Trevor, touché.'

*

In the ensuing weeks, a lot of rumours were going around the art world about the discovery of certain old masterpieces. In both Rome and Paris, everyone in the know was getting more than a little concerned. Meetings were being held in the galleries and museums, including the Louvre, and art deals were suspended as the so-called experts sought to find out which was a forgery and which was not! The only good news for Madame Connie was that she got the Van Gogh back, returned to her from the United States. It would, of course, be put back in the secret room along with all the others.

It was at about this time that Anna and Daniel were stopped in the village by two strangers, both men, who insisted they wanted to treat the pair of them to lunch and discuss something that could be to their advantage. Daniel refused until he was assured that it was all above board and they would come to no harm. The two men identified themselves as representatives of the Israeli government which Daniel took to mean they were members of Mossad, the Israeli secret service. What on earth did they want with them?

Over lunch the two men, who gave only their first names 'Rudd' and 'Owen', explained they had received reports to indicate that many of the paintings stolen during World War II had finished up in the château where Anna and Daniel worked.

It was a long lunch and Anna and Daniel left with mixed feelings, both wondering what they should do. They had been asked to do something that did not come naturally to either of them: the betrayal of their mistress who had, for the most part, been very good to them. Rudd and Owen had insisted that it was morally justified; they needed help to return the paintings to the people to whom they properly belonged: the people of Israel.

As they made their way back to the château, Daniel

and Anna who, given her Jewish roots was in even more of a quandary than Daniel, talked earnestly. They were still undecided what to do as they entered the building.

It was a dark, moonless night in December when things happened in the château. The rain that hammered on the old building seemed to spell out a false sense of security, for no one would be out in this weather – not even thieves, Connie thought to herself, snuggling under the bedcovers and wishing Arthur Thomas had not so cruelly betrayed her. She could have done with his muscular presence right here and now – she could have done with the thirty million euros even more, for she had finally got that information out of Paul. How could AT do that to her? How could he? Connie chided herself with a nervous laugh, but she lay awake for quite a while before finally drifting off to sleep.

Anna and Daniel, having at last decided what they would do, had contacted Rudd and arrangements had been put in place. As agreed, that night they left the small side door open as they retired. Some hours later, four hooded, shadowy figures with blackened faces quietly entered the library. Opening the concealed door, they stood for a stunned moment surveying the impressive sight laid out before them. Within minutes, the room was emptied of its contents. The last thing they did before leaving was to deface the spaces where the paintings had hung, as if to say – you have held them long enough but now they are being returned to their rightful owners. Then they were gone.

The disappearance of the paintings was not discovered for three months, the Countess having lost interest in disposing of them. It had been during a routine inspection that the hidden room was opened and found to be empty. All the staff were detained for questioning and then released. None of them knew anything about it. The paintings were stolen many months ago, they said, and hadn't been seen since – apart from one that had been recovered in America.

Convinced of their innocence and taking the view that the Countess was time-wasting, the police dropped the investigation although not before they had, on Connie's insistence, traced and interviewed Greta Geist.

Unfortunately, Greta thought she was being accused of murder and, panicking, blamed her lover Mata who promptly accused her of Otto's demise. Either way, they both ended up in the female wing of the same jail that now held two other would-be owners of Connie's precious paintings. Everything had certainly come around again and not at all to the four prisoners' liking. As far as Jonathan and Dudley were concerned, they would be out after ten years. It seemed that stealing paintings was considered to be only marginally less serious a crime than shooting someone.

When all the excitement had died down and normal life at the château had resumed, a letter addressed to all the staff came in the mail one day. In it were details of large sums of money that had been paid into their individual bank accounts. It was almost as if they had won a share in the National Lottery – perhaps they had. It was very generous to say the least, but with thirty million euros in his pocket, their benefactor could afford to be. Anna smiled as she noted the signature on the bottom of the letter, with the words: 'Love from AT and Mrs Susan Stevens. Mum's the word!'

It seemed the wily farmer had got his wish: his beloved daughter had married into a rich family and he for one would not have to get up to milk his cows again. As far as his new son-in-law was concerned, he found the promised fruit had most definitely been worth the wait.

In Windsor, Cassie had forgiven Tom for the curtains and, now that they had a bigger house and garden, he was able to have the pet he had always wanted: a dog named Spike. Spike was not the only addition to the contented Rendell family: Cassie was pregnant again and both she and Tom were overjoyed.

Connie was overjoyed too; she had found a new chauffeur who left her breathless and exhausted each night, just the way she liked it. She did eventually receive from the Vatican the balance for the Mona Lisa. Thirty million euros would help to keep her in the manner she richly deserved – or so she thought – but to anyone who might be tempted to accept an invitation to sell anything at the château – whether it be paintings, buildings, cars or even paper clips – they might well be advised to book in at the local bed and breakfast – not that it would make any difference for, as Tom Rendell could have told them, whatever Madame Connie wants, she normally gets!